$\mathcal{P}$icturing $\mathcal{A}$lyssa

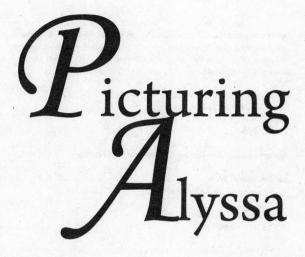

Picturing Alyssa

A NOVEL

Alison Lohans

DUNDURN
TORONTO

Project Editor: Michael Carroll
Editor: Jennifer McKnight
Design: Jennifer Scott
Printer: Webcom

Library and Archives Canada Cataloguing in Publication

Lohans, Alison, 1949-
    Picturing Alyssa / Alison Lohans.

Issued also in an electronic format.
ISBN 978-1-55488-925-9

    I. Title.

PS8573.O35P53 2011   jC813'.54   C2010-907302-9

1   2   3   4   5   15   14   13   12   11

We acknowledge the support of the **Canada Council for the Arts** and the **Ontario Arts Council** for our publishing program. We also acknowledge the financial support of the **Government of Canada** through the **Canada Book Fund** and **Livres Canada Books**, and the **Government of Ontario** through the **Ontario Book Publishing Tax Credit** and the **Ontario Media Development Corporation**.

Care has been taken to trace the ownership of copyright material used in this book. The author and the publisher welcome any information enabling them to rectify any references or credits in subsequent editions.

J. Kirk Howard, President

Printed and bound in Canada.
www.dundurn.com

Dundurn
3 Church Street, Suite 500
Toronto, Ontario, Canada
M5E 1M2

Gazelle Book Services Limited
White Cross Mills
High Town, Lancaster, England
LA1 4XS

Dundurn
2250 Military Road
Tonawanda, NY
U.S.A. 14150

This book is dedicated
with much love to my mother

Mildred Standing Lohans

with thanks for sharing your
stories of your childhood.

Acknowledgements

The author would like to express her gratitude to the Saskatchewan Arts Board for the generous funding that assisted with the completion of this book.

Chapter One

"Oh, no!" Alyssa Dixon groaned. The bomb she'd drawn so carefully now had a squiggle on the edge.

"What's wrong?" Her friend Rachel bent over the same poster, printing NO MORE BOMBS! across the top. The dining-room table was covered with art supplies and the *N* volume of the encyclopedia.

"See?" The mistake was so ugly she felt like giving up. Everything was so *hard* these days — ever since January when her baby sister Charlotte was born, dead. Just thinking about it, Alyssa felt heavy and tired. Nothing was the same anymore. Especially Mom.

"Hmm." Rachel tucked her dark frizzy hair behind her ears. "We're going to put the *X* on the bomb...."

"Not *there*." Alyssa chewed the inside of her lip.

Rachel went back to printing. Her red letters were straight and even. "It's not like people will notice," she said. "*I* think it's really good. Nobody would guess that two eleven-year-olds made this."

Alyssa looked toward the hallway. The light was on in the baby's room. That's exactly what Mom would've said before.... She rested her head on the table, watching her friend. Rachel hadn't been over for a while, and it was so good to have company. Rachel's marker made little squeaky sounds. The wet ink smell crept into her nose, waking her up a bit. The way Rachel explained it, the squiggle didn't matter. So how come she'd almost started to cry?

There was a tromping sound on the basement stairs. Ethan's dirty jeans walked through the kitchen and stood by the table. "Are you done?" her older brother asked. He was wearing his black shirt with the orange peace symbol — the same one he'd had on all week. Shaggy brown hair covered his ears. Annoyance flared in Ethan's face. "You're taking too long. I'm not missing the movie because you're slow."

"We're not slow," Alyssa said. She flipped through the pages of the encyclopedia. Finding a map of North America, she quickly sketched the continent on the other piece of cardboard. Ethan had promised to staple their posters to a pole for the peace march tomorrow. Rachel's mom was coming in less than an hour to pick Rachel up — and the poster-pole too.

"Help us, okay?" Rachel thrust the red marker into Ethan's hand. "Make an X over the bomb."

Ethan leaned over the poster. His red lines didn't go anywhere near her mistake, but somehow it didn't look as bad anymore. Rachel was right. The people at the peace march probably wouldn't notice.

A sudden *thump* on the table made her laugh. Marigold, their cat, had jumped up to see what was happening.

"Stupid cat!" Ethan said. Now one of his lines skewed sideways.

Unconcerned, Marigold walked across the poster.

Alyssa opened her arms. "Here, boy," she said, lifting him to rest against her shoulder. A rumbling purr vibrated through Marigold's relaxed, stripey self. Alyssa buried her face in his fur and was rewarded with a cold, wet nose probing her cheek. During the hard times after the baby died, Marigold had been there any time she needed a friend.

"Stupid cat," Ethan said again.

"Use some EZ-White," Rachel suggested.

Alyssa got up and rummaged through the drawer of stationery supplies. It used to be easy to find stuff, but now the contents were a jumble. She dug through a heap of sticky pads and paper clips, rubber bands, twist ties, and old shoelaces. Something sharp poked her finger — a thumbtack, it turned out — as she scattered pencils and erasers, and a pair of red-handled scissors.

"Hurry up!" Ethan said.

"I'm looking!" Was it in the pile on the counter? She moved advertising flyers, cash register receipts, unopened mail, report cards, and an oven mitt. Yuck — there was a brown shriveled apple core. "I can't find it," she said, and sat down.

"I just remembered," Ethan said. "It's in my room." Soon afterwards he plopped the EZ-White onto the table. Marigold sneezed and jumped off the table when Ethan pulled out the smelly little sponge.

Alyssa watched her brother fix his mistake. "Thanks," she mumbled when he handed her the EZ-White. The clocked chimed 7:30 as she painted white over her own squiggle.

"Help me finish North America," Rachel said. She had already coloured the eastern coastline, and now was working her way inland.

Working fast, Alyssa coloured Alaska, then British Columbia and Washington.

"You're taking too long," Ethan complained again.

Rachel tossed him a blue marker. "So help us. Do the Arctic coast. And Greenland."

Ethan's sigh gusted against Alyssa's arm as she coloured. Up by the North Pole, a blue shark took shape and began swimming toward the top of Canada. "*Ethan!*" she yelled.

Ethan grinned. "Maybe I won't colour over it."

She scowled at him — but it would be silly to waste time arguing. Pressing her lower lip between her teeth, she worked on Baja California, then the rest of Mexico.

"Alyssa?" Mom's voice called faintly from the baby's room. "Will you come here, please?"

Alyssa sighed. Was Mom going to bug her about doing the dishes? Now that Dad was doing most of the cooking, he didn't help wash up afterwards. "*Why?*" she yelled.

If her mother answered, Alyssa didn't hear. She didn't like going in the baby's room. It used to be Ethan's bedroom, with posters of humpback whales and hockey players on the grey walls, and the computer on Ethan's desk. Now the room was pink. A teddy bear mobile dangled from the crib. Cheerful little-kid pictures of animals and clowns were on the walls. Alyssa had helped choose them, and she and Mom laughed a lot while putting them up. Mom's big stomach had jiggled when she laughed. "*Ewwww*," Ethan said when Dad asked him to help assemble the changing table, "now my room'll stink like baby poop." But it wasn't Ethan's room anymore — or anybody's room. Mom sat in the new padded rocking chair a lot, doing nothing.

Alyssa got up. If she didn't, Rachel might go instead. "What do you want?" she asked.

"Can you help me with something?"

"*Mom...!* We have to finish the posters." Alyssa sighed and went into the dreaded pink room.

Her mother was kneeling on the floor, dressed in her dirty bathrobe. Her greasy hair dangled in ugly strings, and her face looked like a puffy mask with dark smudges under the eyes. This bedraggled person couldn't be the same Mom who used to be full of smiles and hugs and interesting ideas. She looked nothing like the seventh grade teacher kids liked so much. Rumpled baby clothes lay in heaps on the carpet. Mom sniffled. "Can you help me? I want to get these put away."

Alyssa stared at the bright orange butterflies on the curtains. She couldn't stand seeing Mom's mouth wobbling into strange shapes, or tears streaking down her face. "Just put them in the box," Alyssa said impatiently. A cardboard box was nearby; she gave it a gentle kick toward her mother.

"Please, can you help me?"

Alyssa felt like scooping up the little shirts and sleepers, the booties and bibs and blankets, and just dumping them. Or maybe kicking them all over — except that would be too mean. Why was Mom asking her? Grandma could've done it when she came from Ohio to help, during those first awful weeks. Auntie Deb could've done it when she came after Grandma went home. What about Mom's friends, who'd called so many times? At first, anyhow. Or Dad? "*I'm not ready*," Mom said whenever somebody offered to help put things away. So what made her finally decide to do it?

"Okay." Alyssa sat down and reached for a yellow sleeper with flowers on the front. The tiny sleeves and legs dangled. They should've had little wiggling arms and legs inside them. A lump grew in her throat. Then she just felt … *empty*. Like the sleeper. She dropped it in the cardboard box.

"Fold it," Mom said.

Not "Would you mind folding it?" or "Please fold it, sweetheart." Just "fold it."

"Why?" Alyssa asked. "It's not like —" Just in time, she stopped herself. *It's not like we need them*, she'd almost said.

Mom didn't say anything.

"Alyssa!" Ethan bellowed. "Are you coming?"

"Yes!" Angrily, she crumpled the sleeper, then lined up the sleeves, the legs, with the zipper lying flat.

Beside her, Mom was carefully folding, and then re-folding, a tiny blue-checkered dress.

The phone rang. Ethan's feet stomped to the kitchen to answer it. "Lyssa!" he yelled. "It's for you."

A phone call? Only Rachel ever called. She put the folded sleeper in the cardboard box and ran to pick up the receiver. "Hello?" she said breathlessly.

Somebody giggled. There was a loud liquid *whoosh* followed by a choking, gurgling sound. More giggling. Then the line clicked.

Alyssa's face went hot.

"Who was it?" Rachel asked.

She sat down at the table. "Somebody's toilet," she said.

"I bet it was Brooklynne," Rachel said.

That was something else that was wrong. Brooklynne had been picking on her all year, and it was getting worse.

Ethan set a wooden pole on the table. "Zach's probably waiting," he said. "If you want the posters stapled, I'm doing it now."

Rachel quickly coloured more blue at the top of North America. Ethan's shark almost didn't show any more.

Alyssa handed her brother the poster with the bomb. As she watched him use the staple gun, she wished she could go to the movie too. Once Rachel left, she'd be stuck at home. Like always.

At least tomorrow they'd have the peace march. It was such an important thing to do — and maybe people would notice her. There might be TV cameras — maybe she'd even be on the news!

Chapter Two

It felt weird walking down the middle of Hartford Street — especially going through a red light. Cars honked.

Rachel carried the sign they'd made. The NO MORE BOMBS! looked just as good as some of the other posters. The squiggles didn't show at all. Neither did Ethan's covered-up shark on the other side.

All around them, peace marchers carried banners and placards. Some walked quietly, but others chanted: "One, two, three, four — we don't want another war! Five, six, seven, eight — act with love, instead of hate!" Somebody at the front was tapping a cadence on a drum. It echoed off the buildings in little burps of sound.

Rachel handed her the sign. "Here — my arms are tired."

When Alyssa took it, the sign swayed. She steadied it just before it hit Rachel's mom, Lori, who was talking to a friend.

Alyssa drew in a deep breath. It felt awesome to be doing something as important as the peace march. On TV, the radio, and in the newspapers, everybody was talking about the war. At home, Dad talked about it a lot. In the past, Mom had gone to peace marches too.

"Your mother needs time to grieve," Dad had said one evening when Alyssa was unhappy and Mom didn't notice. She'd worked hard on a speech about protecting the whales. It was memorized, with expression, and she had four posters to illustrate her points. On the way out to recess afterwards, Brooklynne had said to Mackenzie: "Alyssa thinks she's so smart. And ..." She'd whispered something, and the two girls laughed. Then Brooklynne looked straight at her. As if she'd *wanted* her to hear. When she told Dad — instead of Mom — he only patted her back and said, "It sounds like that little girl has some growing up to do." And then he made popcorn.

"How's it going?" Rachel's mom broke into her thoughts.

"We're fine," Rachel said. Then Alyssa stepped on Rachel's trailing shoelace, and they bumped heads as they looked to see what was wrong. Rachel burst into giggles. Ethan looked embarrassed, walking nearby with his friend Zach.

"What do we want?" shouted a man with a megaphone.

"*PEACE!*" the people yelled.

"When do we want it?"

"*NOW!*"

The man said it over and over. Alyssa waved the sign and yelled along with Rachel and her mom.

Mrs. Fraser, their sixth grade teacher, approached on the sidewalk. "Mrs. Fraser!" Alyssa called, and waved.

Their teacher always said it was important to be involved with community activities.

"Hi, Mrs. Fraser!" Rachel's voice was louder. Mrs. Fraser couldn't possibly miss it.

Just for an instant, Mrs. Fraser's eyes met Alyssa's. Alyssa smiled, and waved again. Mrs. Fraser's mouth tightened. She looked at her watch, and walked faster. There was no smile, no sign of recognition.

A huge, sudden hurt quivered in Alyssa's middle.

"I don't get it," Rachel said. "She *saw* us, I know it."

"Don't get what, hon?" asked her mom.

"Mrs. Fraser. She walked right by and didn't even smile." Rachel's feet stamped harder on the pavement.

Lori sighed. "Maybe she's in a hurry. Oh, girls … You know a lot of people don't agree with what we're doing. Mrs. Fraser could be one of them."

Alyssa stamped. Her tight shoes pinched her toes. In class, Mrs. Fraser was strict about the Pledge of Allegiance. She talked a lot about being patriotic.

The drumbeats kept bouncing off buildings. All around, there was the sound of shuffling feet, all these people out in the street because they thought war and violence were wrong.

If Mrs. Fraser didn't agree with the peace marchers, she wouldn't think much of Alyssa's genealogy project. Besides doing a family tree display with photos, everyone was supposed to write a report and give a presentation on things their family had contributed to today's way of life. The only thing Alyssa could think of to talk about was how almost all of her relatives were Quakers, and worked to make the world a more peaceful place. She glanced at Rachel and her mom; they were members of the same Quaker meeting. The trouble was, Mrs. Fraser said she'd give bonus points to people who could show how their ancestors helped protect America's freedom.

Maybe she should change her topic to farming, like Rachel's. Rachel had photos of people using old-fashioned farming equipment. Her great-grandfather invented a combine part. Compared to that, Alyssa's pictures were boring — people in long rows.

The peace marchers turned onto Twelfth Avenue, and walked past City Hall. Another light turned red, and they kept right on walking. Everywhere, cars and pedestrians had to wait.

Alyssa's toenails hurt. She tried walking on her heels and grabbed Rachel's arm when she teetered off balance.

"What're you doing that for?" Rachel asked.

"Feet hurt," Alyssa muttered.

Rachel's mom took the sign from her. "Are you okay, Alyssa?"

"My shoes are tight." Embarrassed, she walked normally again and hoped Lori wouldn't notice Ethan's shoes flapping. One day he'd shown her the way the soles had separated. A little rock was stuck in the funny-shaped stuff inside, and he'd used a screwdriver to pry it out. Ethan needed new shoes too.

They arrived at the park where the march started. As the crowd dispersed, some teenagers went by carrying signs that looked like they'd been done in a hurry. One of the girls had purple hair. She stopped to look at their sign. "Great posters," she said. "It's cool that kids care."

"Thanks," Alyssa said shyly.

"I love your hair!" Rachel yelled as the girl ran to catch up with her friends. She tugged at her frizzy hair. "Mom? Can I dye my hair?"

"You wish!" Lori laughed and got the car keys out of her fanny pack.

It was hard, watching the easy way Rachel and her mom acted together. Alyssa banged the end of the sign post on the sidewalk. Why couldn't she live at Rachel's house?

When Alyssa got home, she poured herself a bowl of cereal and turned on the TV.

Ethan flopped into the reclining chair. "How come you're watching golf?" he asked. "You always say it's boring."

"It is." She set her bowl on the couch cushion. "But it's better than boxing — or car races."

Ethan pushed his hair out of his eyes. "How'd you like the march?"

"Fun." There hadn't been any TV cameras, which was too bad. And then she remembered Mrs. Fraser. "I saw Mrs. Fraser. I know she saw us — but she didn't even smile!"

"Huh. Maybe she didn't recognize you?"

"She *did!*" Alyssa fidgeted with the remote. The golf tournament flicked into pictures of a desert village.

There were tanks and soldiers and wrecked buildings. Frightened people so skinny you could see the bones in their faces.

"That's so sick!" Ethan's grey eyes were hot with anger. "We wouldn't want anybody doing that to us. Like they even have a chance!" He stomped to the basement, and Alyssa could hear his loose soles flapping.

On TV, buildings and cars exploded and tanks drove through dusty streets. Scared-looking people hid behind doorways and ledges. Others looked so upset and angry that she almost cried. Did Mrs. Fraser think it was okay to kill civilians? *Kids?* There were children with bandages. There were also kids with guns who were trying to help protect their families.

She clicked the remote. Maybe her genealogy project *was* a good idea. How could she talk to the class about making peace?

Alyssa lay down on the living-room floor. A long strand of spider web dangled between the ceiling and the framed painting of a winter farmyard scene. There were fence posts in the foreground, with puffy snow on top. Tall, dried grass poked through the snow. Animal tracks circled around and then went into a clump of trees. Further back, there was a barn and a silo, and a wagon with big, old-fashioned wheels. The painting had been there for as long as Alyssa could remember.

She went to the bookcase for the heavy blue family book with all the Quaker relatives. She got shoeboxes of photos from the cupboard, then found the magnifying glass.

The old family photos were so boring, black-and-white people standing in lines. The names were on the backs in faded ink, in hard-to-read old-fashioned writing. There was somebody's Grandfather Standing and Great-Aunt Florence, in a wheelchair, dated 1921. Another photo dated 1920 showed children, parents, and old people. These pictures didn't tell any kind of story. And Mrs. Fraser wanted a story.

There was a thud. Alyssa looked up and saw that Marigold had knocked one of the shoeboxes onto the floor. Photographs were scattered everywhere. In the midst of them, he seemed to be stalking something. Maybe there'd been a bug in the box? Alyssa brushed away golden cat hairs and started scooping up the pictures.

Marigold stepped into her lap, purring, thrusting his whiskery face against her cheek.

"You're silly," she said, stroking him. There was something so incredibly *ordinary*, so calming, about him, and his unblinking green-gold eyes. As she reached for one last photo, Marigold batted it. Now there was a tiny jagged hole in one of the corners. "Bad cat!" she said.

Marigold gave her a dirty look and walked away, tail held high.

Alyssa took a closer look at the photograph. This one showed a family outside a house — a dad, a mom, a big brother and sister. Four little kids sat on a bench. One of the boys looked mischievous. And ... it was weird, but the oldest girl seemed to be looking right at her.

Who was she? On the back it said *Dallas County, Iowa, 1931*. The parents were George and Martha

Clayton. The girl, beside her mother, was Deborah. The oldest brother was Wilfred. The kids on the bench were Herbert, Frances, Eva, and Charles.

Alyssa reached for the magnifying glass. Deborah Clayton came sharply into focus. The shape of her face was completely familiar. Alyssa's heart beat faster. The girl seemed to be smiling — though her mouth was straight. Was the magnifying glass playing tricks on her eyes?

A peculiar tingling started in the back of Alyssa's head, and quickly spread. Everything blurred. She tried to stand, but couldn't. "*Mom!*" she tried to yell. Darkness swooshed around her. With a hard *bump* she fell backwards.

Tree branches rustled in the breeze. Birds were singing. Nearby, she could hear ... *chickens?* Further away, crows cawed. And there were cows. Long grass tickled her neck and face.

Alyssa opened her eyes and sat up.

Chapter Three

The air smelled different, a farm kind of smell. Brown chickens, black chickens, and a few black-and-white speckled ones walked around on the grass nearby. On her left there was a weather-beaten shed. A loud squawking came from inside it. A chicken came out, ruffling its brown feathers as it waddled down a little ramp.

Alyssa's heart beat hard and fast. *Where was she?* She squeezed her eyes shut so tightly that her eyeballs hurt. The chicken sounds didn't go away. Neither did the big fly that kept landing on her arm. In the distance, a cow mooed.

She stood up. The chickens closest to her squawked in alarm. In almost a single motion, they flowed toward the shed — all of them except one with long black tail feathers that curved in a tight rainbow shape. That chicken flapped its wings, clucking loudly. Its comb was large and red, and wobbled. Alyssa backed up. The big bird glared at her with beady yellow eyes; its clucking had an ominous sound. With a sudden *whoosh* it flew at her.

Alyssa yelled and covered her face. Wings flapped. Claws scratched her arms. A sharp beak pecked at her. It was like being caught in a feathery tornado. She tried pushing the chicken away, but it was strong, and fierce.

It seemed to go on forever. Until, suddenly, she had help. "Shoo!" someone said. "Stop it!"

Miraculously, it stopped. The chicken strutted off, clucking angrily. Stunned, Alyssa looked at the red scratches and peck marks on her arms.

"He's a mean old rooster." Her rescuer was holding a broom. He was about eight years old and wore jeans overalls. He was barefoot.

"Thanks," she stammered.

Curious brown eyes studied her. "What's thee doing out here with the chickens?" the boy asked.

"I don't know." Her brain frantically tried to piece it together. The dizzy spell, the blackout. Waking up outside in a place she'd never been. She rubbed her smarting arms.

A crow cawed. Alyssa jumped at the harsh sound overhead. Not too far away a house stood near a clump of trees; a rope swing hung from one of them. There was a barn and a silo. A windmill. A garden. Green fields rose and fell in rolling hills.

The boy's forehead puckered. Freckles splashed across his nose and cheeks. "I didn't see thee on the road," he said. "How'd thee get here? Did thee come through the pasture?"

Something clicked into place. She'd thought the boy had been saying "the" too much — but he was calling her *thee*. That was how Quakers had talked, a long time ago.

"Where is this?" she asked desperately. "I just … I was on the couch, looking at a picture. Then I got dizzy, and — *yikes!* — suddenly I'm here."

The boy gave her a skeptical look and swished the broom through the long grass. "It's our farm."

A chill stirred the hairs on Alyssa's arms. "But *where?* I have to figure out how to get home." Judging from the weird way she'd arrived, going home wouldn't be easy. It seemed like the picture had brought her here — but it was still on the couch, probably.

"I can tell thee's not from here." The boy looked uncomfortable. "Chatham's the nearest town. Chatham, Iowa," he added, at Alyssa's blank look.

Iowa? "I live in North Dakota," she said faintly.

"How'd thee come so far?" the boy asked. "Did thee take the train?"

"I *told* you …" Alyssa swallowed hard at a sudden dryness in her throat. "I was sitting on the couch, looking at a picture, and …" What if she couldn't go back home? How long would it be before Ethan — or Mom — noticed that she wasn't there?

"They're back," the boy said. He took off, running, toward the house.

It had to be a dream. Maybe she'd fallen asleep. Except …

A dog barked. Alyssa looked in that direction and saw an old-fashioned car parked in the driveway. Near it, a man and a tall boy were getting out of a carriage that was hitched up to two horses — big brown ones with dark, swishing tails. A black-and-white dog danced around the people.

Then the dog noticed her. Barking, it bounded across the expanse of grass. Alyssa shrank away from it. "Flossie!" someone shouted.

In the next instant Flossie greeted her, with tail wagging hard. Alyssa let out a relieved breath and petted the dog as it jumped against her, sniffing her hands, her jeans, then her shoes.

"Flossie! Get down." An older girl hurried over.

The boy ran beside her. "See?" he said. "I told thee so! That old rooster was attacking her."

"I'm sorry." The girl apologized profusely. She seemed to be trying not to stare. Alyssa studied her carefully. Her dress came to below her knees and was printed with small yellow-and-brown flowers. It had elbow-length sleeves and buttons down the front. The girl was barefoot.

"She's from North Dakota," the boy announced.

Another voice intruded. "Herbert, did thee bring in the water and the eggs?" The man walked toward them. Obviously the children's father, he wore jeans and a blue shirt with long sleeves rolled up to his elbows.

The boy looked embarrassed. "I forgot."

The father, too, seemed puzzled by her appearance. His tanned face looked kind; brown eyes regarded her from behind wire-rimmed glasses. "My name's Alyssa Dixon," she said to him. "I don't know how I got here."

"She says she's from North Dakota." Herbert rumpled Flossie's ears.

"Do thy chores, Herbert. Thee mustn't keep thy mother waiting any longer."

Herbert picked up the broom and walked away, followed by the dog. The older boy joined them.

Self-conscious, Alyssa looked at the girl.

Grey eyes regarded her from a face that seemed oddly familiar. Straight brown hair was held back from her face by clips, and fluttered in the breeze. "Alyssa," the girl said softly. "What an interesting name."

Alyssa stuffed her hands in her jeans pockets. "What year is this?" she asked desperately. Without warning, the back of her head tingled. Her eyes blurred. She felt so dizzy she was afraid she might throw up.

Darkness came.

This time cushions broke her fall. She was on the couch. At home.

"Alyssa! You know better than to jump on the furniture!"

She blinked. "I ..."

Mom's grey eyes held the flat, empty look that had been there since that day at the hospital when everything changed. The same old flannel nightgown dangled beneath her housecoat, and she was wearing the same pair of Dad's black socks she'd had on yesterday. Cat hairs clung to the toes and insteps. Mom was holding the picture.

What had happened? Red scratches and peck marks smarted on both of her arms. "I was just looking at that picture, and suddenly ..." It wasn't going to make sense.

Mom sighed. "This picture was on the couch — wedged partway between the cushions. These are family mementoes, Alyssa. If you're not going to treat them right …" She gestured at the shoe box on the floor, filled with jumbled photographs.

"I'm sorry," she muttered. If Mom wasn't even going to ask what had happened — how she just appeared, out of nowhere — there was nothing much she could say.

"Put that stuff away." Her mother's irritated voice pricked at something deep inside her. "Then go clean your room." Mom rubbed her forehead, flipping back her greasy hair. She put the picture of the Clayton family on top of the other photos. Her heavy footsteps disappeared in the direction of the baby's room — as usual. The sounds of Ethan's music came from downstairs, along with the *sproings* and explosions from his computer game.

Alyssa's mouth wobbled. Was *this* a dream, instead? A horrible nightmare that just wouldn't stop? Woodenly, she put the heavy family book back in its place on the shelf, then lugged the boxes of photos over to the cupboard where they belonged. Saving the picture with a cat-claw hole in one corner, she went down the hall to her room.

On her bed, Marigold greeted her with a soft *mrraau*. Alyssa plopped down, and pulled him into her lap. Vibrating with a loud purr, he rubbed his head against her. Alyssa's knotted insides loosened. She stroked Marigold's rounded head and cool, pointed ears.

Abruptly, the cat stopped purring. He sniffed her forearms. Then his raspy tongue licked one of the scratches. "At least *you* noticed," she said. In the mirror she saw tangled brown hair and a face that looked confused. She didn't look anything like the picture of herself tucked in the corner. In that picture, taken last fall, she was holding Marigold. She was smiling as if nothing bad ever happened. Now, her lavender t-shirt looked like it belonged in the laundry. It was a good thing Brooklynne couldn't see her.

Mom said to clean her room. Well ... lined notebook pages were strewn across her science and social studies texts, which happened to be on the floor. Dirty clothes lay on the floor too. Glasses with milk dried in the bottoms sat on her chest of drawers and on the little table by her bed. Mom must've looked.

Again she could hear the snappish sound of her mother's voice and see that look in her eyes that pushed everybody away. As if nobody but the baby was important. What about the missed meals and the clothes that didn't get washed? Why should she clean her room when Mom wasn't doing *her* jobs?

In class, Mrs. Fraser talked about writing down experiences and feelings, and how it could help you understand yourself and other people better. She should write about how grouchy Mom was.

Alyssa picked up some paper. Choosing a pen with green ink, she lay flat on her stomach. What did you call a weird experience like what had just happened? She listed a few things:

- *Picture, looking at girl*

- *Falling*
- *Rooster, chickens*
- *Farm*
- *Boy, Herbert*
- *Girl*

Dad had just come home; she could hear his foot-steps tromping through the house and his voice calling "Hello?" Ethan yelled back from the basement. Alyssa tapped the end of the pen against her teeth. The click-ing sound made her feel more … *here*, somehow. Dad wouldn't expect her to answer.

The footsteps headed for the kitchen. Then the refrigerator door banged shut. "Jennifer?" Dad said. "Did you go shopping today?"

If Mom replied, Alyssa didn't hear.

There was the sound of a pan coming out of the stove drawer. Water ran in the kitchen sink. "Alyssa?" Dad called.

She opened her bedroom door. "What?"

"Come into the kitchen," Dad said. "I shouldn't have to shout."

Alyssa scuffed her way along the hall. The framed baby pictures of her and Ethan were crooked. With her finger, she traced lines in the dust.

Dad's face had a grumpy, tired look. The counter was full of dirty dishes and an empty milk jug. "There you are," Dad said. "I'd like you to go to Bristow's and bring back some milk, cheese, and ground beef. Oh — and some eggs and bread, too. And apples."

31

The little corner store was five blocks away. Mom didn't shop there because everything cost more. Alyssa looked at Dad and decided not to mention that. "How will I get there?" she asked.

Dad let out a loud, angry huff. "Walk. Take your bike. Fly. Just do it, please — unless you want to fix supper yourself?" He started dumping dishes in the sink. Silverware and plates and plastic glasses clattered against each other.

"Why can't Ethan go?" After she'd said it, she wished she hadn't.

Dad turned the water on hard. "Ethan went last time." His blue eyes stared right at her, making her feel ashamed. It had been easier when Grandma Hadley was here. She'd come all the way from Ohio the same day Mom got home from the hospital. Things had felt *almost* right with Grandma around.

"Sorry," she said.

Dad gave her a little smile as he took twenty dollars from his wallet. Then he squirted detergent into the sink with the dirty dishes. "One of these days Mom will feel more like herself," he said.

When? Alyssa didn't ask. She put the twenty dollars in her jacket pocket, and reached for her backpack. The door banged behind her.

Her bike tires scrunched against the pavement as she rode along the quiet street. Leaves were starting to come out on the bare branches. A few hedges had pink and white blossoms, and their sweet flowery scent wafted out as she pedaled by. But ... goose bumps shivered her arms in spite of her warm jacket sleeves. That other place — *Iowa?* There, it had been summer. How could that be? Maybe she'd imagined it after all....

The handlebars jolted. Her bike flew sideways. Alyssa caught a glimpse of the pothole she'd just hit, a big one. Then she was on the ground with one leg stuck through the frame of her bike. Her elbow jangled with shooting electric pains.

Somebody laughed.

Not Brooklynne! Blinking back tears, she lurched to her feet and pushed off as fast as she could. Bristow's Market was only a few doors away.

"Better watch where you're going, loser," Brooklynne yelled.

Alyssa clenched her teeth. She pedaled hard, then parked her bike by the store entrance. Maybe Brooklynne would be gone when she came out.

Chapter Four

Bristow's Market felt small and crowded. The lights weren't as bright as in the supermarket or at the food co-op where they bought eggs, honey, dry beans, and flour. At Bristow's the linoleum floor was worn and cracked.

Alyssa walked up and down the aisles. Her elbow still hurt. Vegetable smells drifted around her. The lettuce looked droopy. One of the bags of flour had leaked onto the shelf. Some of the cat food cans had dust on the tops.

"Can I help you find something?" the clerk asked after a while.

"Um —" Alyssa counted on her fingers, trying to remember Dad's list. "Some cheese. And eggs. And milk," she added when she remembered the empty jug on the counter. It seemed like Dad had said more than that, but these would be tricky enough to carry on her bike.

The woman gave her a strange look.

The shelves around her were stocked with dry cereal. Anybody would know that the milk wouldn't be there! The eggs and cheese, either. Alyssa hurried to the refrigerated section. Did the woman think she was going to steal something? But who'd steal cornflakes? The good stuff was all at the front.

And so was Brooklynne, with her perfect straight blond hair and her pink top that hugged her perfect shape. She was looking at the chocolate bars.

Alyssa ducked around the next aisle, full of canned beans and spaghetti. When she edged her way to the cash register, Brooklynne was paying for a Hershey Bar and a Snickers.

The milk was heavy; Alyssa wished she'd used a cart. With one jug dangling from each hand, and the two egg cartons and the cheese scrunched against her sides, she had a sudden, ominous feeling. The cheese plopped down, chunky and orange on the floor. As Alyssa knelt to get it, one white egg and then another fell onto the linoleum with a *splat*. Her face burned.

"Uh oh. Let me help you, dear." The clerk knelt beside her. Plump hands lifted the jugs of milk onto the counter.

"I'm sorry!" Alyssa stammered as she fumbled with the egg cartons. Luckily only two eggs had broken.

"Don't worry about it," the woman said. "These things happen." She cleaned up the mess until only a big wet spot was left.

Brooklynne was still there, watching. She was eating the Hershey Bar.

Alyssa looked away, but not before she'd seen Brooklynne's smirk. She reached in her jacket pocket to pay.

The twenty-dollar bill from Dad wasn't there. Panicking, she checked her other pockets but found nothing. She knew it wasn't in her backpack. The money must've fallen out when she fell off her bike.

"I lost the money," she mumbled. "Can I call my dad?"

There was a sigh as the woman slid a telephone across the counter. Holding her breath, Alyssa punched in the numbers.

"That's twenty dollars, Alyssa!" Dad said when she explained. "You're old enough to be responsible." Brooklynne still lingered by the door. There was a predatory look in her hazel eyes.

"I fell off my bike," Alyssa said in a low voice. "That's when it probably fell out."

"Then go back and look for it," Dad said impatiently.

"But the lady's waiting." Alyssa's hands were sweaty. "Please, could you come?"

The line clicked.

Ethan came instead of Dad. By that time Brooklynne was gone. The clerk had whisked the phone back behind the counter, and was busy marking things on a list. They paid for the groceries and went home exactly the way Alyssa had come. There was no twenty-dollar bill lying in the street.

For supper they had scrambled eggs with cheese and milk. Nothing else.

The next day at school, every time Alyssa was near her, Brooklynne whispered to Mackenzie and then they giggled. Sometimes Chelsea and Jessica joined in too.

It got worse in language arts the day Mrs. Fraser asked them to role-play words for strong emotions. Alyssa and Rachel slid their desks together to plan how to act out "patriotic." It wasn't very nice of Mrs. Fraser to give them a word like that, after the way she'd ignored them at the peace march.

Alyssa's stomach twisted, remembering. Under the flag, a picture of the president was surrounded by shiny foil stars. Across the top of the next bulletin board were big red, white, and blue letters that said PROTECTING OUR DEMOCRACY — LET FREEDOM RING. Below was a display of war medals. Mrs. Fraser had put up the medals her father earned fighting in Vietnam, and some from her grandfather from the Second World War. She'd invited everyone in class to bring medals to put up, and now there were some from the Korean War, the First World War — and even one from the Civil War.

"Do you think she did it on purpose?" Rachel whispered. "Everyone else got fun words."

All around the room, small groups of kids were talking and laughing. "Eggs!" Brooklynne said two rows away. The awful snickering started. Alyssa's face burned.

Rachel nudged her. "What's with Brooklynne?"

Alyssa tucked her feet around the desk legs. She hadn't told Rachel what happened at Bristow's. "I don't know." There was something else she hadn't told Rachel, either. How could you explain about going from your couch to a whole different state a long time ago? Across the aisle, Tristan and Kai pretended to stab each other. "I wish *we* had 'murderous rage,'" she said.

Rachel giggled. "That's not very Quakerly. What would your mom say?"

Alyssa smiled. "She'd figure out a nonviolent way to show it." PATRIOTIC, she printed across the top of her notebook page, copying from the dictionary. "1. loving one's country. 2. showing love and loyal support of one's country." There was nothing wrong with that. But what could you say if your country was doing something that seemed terribly wrong?

Rachel's peridot birthstone ring winked light green as she wrote something lower down the page: "Not fair!" with a frowny face in the middle of the O. Alyssa couldn't help laughing.

"Splat!" Brooklynne's voice was louder.

Moving only her eyes, Alyssa checked on her. The other girl was staring right at her, waiting.

Mrs. Fraser was at the back of the room. "Think about what 'despair' really means, Seth. How would you feel if something terrible was happening and you couldn't do anything to stop it?"

That was easy. All you had to do was think about the Middle East. Or how it felt when you were expecting a new baby, and ...

Rachel seemed to know what she was thinking. "Want to see if Seth will trade words?"

Alyssa shook her head. "Mrs. Fraser wouldn't let us."

"Embarrassed," Mackenzie whispered loudly, and giggled.

"Alyssa *loves* eggs," Brooklynne added.

Rachel's mouth dropped open. "What's she talking

about? Just because her mom's the news anchor now, and her dad's the mayor — what right does that give her to be so snotty?"

Alyssa stabbed her pen through the definition of "patriotic." Mom and Dad, and the other adults at Quaker meeting, talked about how everybody had a little bit of God in them. How it was important to think about that goodness, and try to find it. Well, Brooklynne was different. She didn't have any.

"Class." Mrs. Fraser moved decisively toward Brooklynne and Mackenzie. "Time's almost up. In five minutes we'll begin with Brooklynne and Mackenzie. Are you girls ready?"

Rachel poked her. "What're we going to do?"

Alyssa shrugged. "The flag salute?"

"That'll work," Rachel agreed.

While their teacher talked to Tristan and Kai, Alyssa hurried to the bookshelf to get the *I* encyclopedia. There was just enough time to check some things about Iowa. She looked at pictures of fields of corn and sunflowers, and a big state fair. She looked at the Mississippi River and how it made the eastern state boundary into a curvy line, and how the straighter Missouri River made the western border. Where was Chatham? There it was, a tiny dot west of Des Moines. As fast as she could, Alyssa scanned the pages.

"Class, your time is up." Mrs. Fraser's voice broke her concentration. "All right, Brooklynne and Mackenzie. Let's see what you've planned."

At the front of the room, with their straight, shiny

hair and their perfect tops and jeans, Brooklynne and Mackenzie looked like they could be on TV. "You have to guess our word." Brooklynne's braces flashed when she smiled, a smile that looked like her mom's when she did the six o'clock news. She went to stand behind Mrs. Fraser's desk. "I'm a store lady," she announced.

Alyssa went cold. Rachel poked her. "*Store lady?*" she whispered. "What kind of vocabulary is that?"

Mackenzie walked toward the desk. She was hunched over, and her arms curved out as if she were carrying something heavy.

"May I help you?" Brooklynne's voice had the syrupy tone that telemarketers used.

"Uh ..." Mackenzie pretended to stagger.

Brooklynne hurried to the chalkboard. "SPLAT!!!" she wrote in big letters. Then she turned on Mackenzie. "How could you be so stupid? Dropping eggs all over the floor! You have to pay for them, you know."

Alyssa's heart pounded so hard she was afraid it might explode.

"I'm s-s-s-sorry," Mackenzie stammered. She dropped to her knees and covered her face. Somebody laughed.

"Where's the money?" Brooklynne demanded.

Mackenzie fumbled through her pockets. "I-I ... I-lost it."

It wasn't fair! The way they were doing it, Mrs. Fraser would never guess. Alyssa's hand clenched around her pen. Her shoulders felt tight. Her neck felt tight. Keeping her head down, she wished she could be a rock, a rock that couldn't see or hear. Because if she even looked at Rachel, she'd cry.

Brooklynne triumphantly faced the class. "What's our word?" she asked sweetly.

People clapped and laughed, and shouted out answers: "Mad!" "Clumsy!" "Stupid!" "Sad!"

In a sudden lull, Rachel looked over at Alyssa. "Bullying," she said.

Or being victimized, Alyssa didn't say. It was just too much! Tears raced down her face. She held the open encyclopedia in front of her.

"Alyssa." Mrs. Fraser's voice prodded her. "Are you with us?"

Frantically, Alyssa wiped her eyes on her arm and lowered the book just enough so she could see Mrs. Fraser.

"Put down the encyclopedia, Alyssa," Mrs. Fraser said gently. "I'm sure you'd like everyone else to show you the respect of paying full attention to *your* presentation."

There was a muffled snicker, but everybody else was quiet.

"Brooklynne and Mackenzie," Mrs. Fraser continued, "this was a very convincing presentation." She glanced at the clock. "Was this based on something that actually happened? I'd like to discuss it with you at recess."

There was a shriek of laughter. Giggles erupted from different parts of the room.

"Class!" Mrs. Fraser's angry voice brought instant silence.

The recess bell rang.

As people rummaged in their desks, Alyssa felt Rachel's tap on her arm. "What's all this about?" Rachel demanded.

Alyssa sighed. She couldn't keep putting Rachel off. Not trusting her voice, she wrote in her notebook: "It happened to me at Bristow's. Brooklynne was there — she followed me after I fell off my bike."

Rachel gasped. "That *witch!*"

Alyssa nodded. She ripped out the page and crumpled it.

Brooklynne shot her a poisonous look.

At home, as usual, Mom didn't notice when Alyssa washed the dishes and changed the cat litter without even being asked.

A week went by. Alyssa still didn't know what to do for her genealogy project. She thought about writing to Grandma Hadley. Mrs. Fraser had said letter writing was one way of doing research. Should she write to Great-Grandmother Newlin? Alyssa had never met her, but every October, right on time, a birthday card came in the mail. Great-Grandmother Newlin was really old and lived in a seniors' home in Iowa.

Writing letters seemed like so much work. Email would be faster. Grandma had email, but she didn't check it often. Great-Grandmother Newlin probably didn't know how to use a computer. Maybe she could phone?

The genealogy project was due in two weeks. As usual, there was math homework, creative writing, health, science, and book reports. Alyssa put off thinking about her assignment until Sunday when she and Dad and Ethan were sitting in their Quaker meeting for worship.

Their Quaker meeting was small and didn't own a building, so they rented space downtown in the North Dakota Crop Insurance office. Mom had stayed home with her stringy hair and stained housecoat, and the heavy, sad cloud that was with her all the time. As Alyssa sat wiggling her toes in her tight shoes, she was suddenly glad Mom wasn't there. Sometimes Mom cried in meeting, and Rachel's mom and the other women would hug her afterwards. It was too embarrassing.

Sitting quietly, Alyssa pretended she didn't have a mother. It would be just her and Ethan and Dad. They'd go to school and take care of the house. On weekends, they'd go exciting places like the Mall of the Americas and Disney World. They'd be in lots of peace marches too.

There were fourteen people at meeting, counting two-year-old Mariah who was running around with her doll. Alyssa looked at each person. Ethan's laces were untied, and anybody could see how his shoes were coming apart. Dad sat with his eyes closed. Alyssa noticed, to her horror, that Dad had some white hair! Was he getting old? To stop thinking about that, Alyssa looked at Rachel. A photocopier was behind her, and on the wall, a calendar with a picture of a green-and-yellow tractor. Rachel was twisting her birthstone ring, probably to make the peridot sparkle. *Look at me!* Alyssa thought.

Except for Mariah, with her thumping feet and her baby talk, the room was still. Alyssa shifted in her folding chair. It squeaked. She propped her feet on the rungs. The chair squeaked again.

In meeting for worship, the grownups tried to "center down." That meant being so quiet, and listening so deeply, that you could connect with the bit of God that was inside you, also known as the "Inner Light." There was no minister. Once in a while somebody said something into the quietness. Rachel said her mom loved meeting for worship because it was so peaceful. Alyssa thought it was boring.

Alyssa could hear the pages rustle as Warren Stanley opened a little book and read a question about seeking the goodness in other people. Right away, she quit listening. Warren Stanley didn't know Brooklynne. That made her think about Mrs. Fraser and the genealogy project. Since Mrs. Fraser didn't like talking about peace, maybe she should make something up.

The Underground Railroad! Everybody knew Quakers had helped slaves escape to Canada. Alyssa couldn't remember Mom ever talking about her ancestors helping with the Underground Railroad — but so what?

Was this what the Inner Light was like? An idea coming out of the blue? Except, God wouldn't help people cheat....

Alyssa wiggled. Her chair squeaked again, loudly. Little Mariah laughed. Across the room, Rachel looked like she was about to laugh too.

The Underground Railroad was perfect! Even if it wasn't true. Mom would never find out.

Chapter Five

Another week passed. Then it was Friday, and Alyssa was glad. Rachel had invited her for a sleepover. First, they were going to see *Stardancer*. This would be the perfect time to tell Rachel about the picture and what had happened. The more she thought about it, the more she wondered if she'd somehow made it up. The photograph and the magnifying glass were in her backpack.

The movie theatre was crowded. *Stardancer* was about a superhero who got her powers from the star Betelgeuse. Her daytime cover was as Catherine Richardson, a dancing student at the Omaha Academy of Dance, but any time a danger signal was transmitted through the celestial ether, Stardancer would fly away to trap heinous criminals.

After buying a large buttered popcorn with cheese and onion powder on top and giant soft drinks, Alyssa and Rachel squeezed their way into the last empty seats in the second row from the front. Alyssa laughed as an icy dribble of orange pop trailed down her hand. "Yuk," she said. "Got a napkin?"

"Nope," Rachel said.

"Oh well." The popcorn smelled so good Alyssa couldn't wait. She ate a handful and licked the awesome cheesy-buttery-onion off her fingers.

"Hi, Alyssa. Hi Rachel."

Rachel turned to look, so Alyssa had to turn around too. Brooklynne sat there with her perfect, straight blond hair. Brooklynne's mouth was smiling with her silvery braces showing, but her eyes looked mean. As usual, Mackenzie was beside her.

"Hi," Rachel said flatly, and faced forward again.

"Hi," Alyssa said, hating how she sounded like an echo of Rachel.

"Have you got anything in your pockets, Alyssa?" Brooklynne's voice was syrupy sweet, exactly like the way she'd spoken in that horrible skit.

Heat rushed into Alyssa's face. Rachel nudged her. "Just ignore her," she whispered. On the big screen there was a quiz question about who played the leading role in the latest Harry Potter movie.

"Did you find your twenty dollars, Alyssa?" Brooklynne persisted.

Alyssa gasped. How had Brooklynne known it was a twenty? Unless ... Anger shot through her. What would Mom do? Mom wouldn't let Brooklynne get away with this! "Is there any other place we can sit?" she whispered to Rachel. As usual, Brooklynne and Mackenzie were snickering.

Rachel shook her head. "Don't let on that they're getting to you — they'll only make it worse next time."

Next time. Always, there'd be a next time. Alyssa held herself straight and proud. Next year, in junior high, there'd be more kids. Brooklynne might not even be in any of her classes. And maybe Brooklynne would find somebody else to torment.

The lights dimmed. There was a reminder for people to turn off their cell phones. A waving American flag appeared on the screen. The president's voice boomed through the theatre, talking about terrorists and evil things that were happening in the Middle East. Alyssa squirmed in her seat, wishing she could turn it off like the TV at home. People in the theatre were clapping. "Nuke 'em!" somebody yelled.

After previews for a spy movie and a film about frog heroes who wanted to become knights, *Stardancer* finally began. Alyssa got caught up in the story of Catherine, who was a beautiful dancer and always tried harder than anyone else at the Omaha Academy of Dance, but another girl, Allegra, always got the starring roles. One day Allegra tripped Catherine during a performance. Catherine's foot was injured badly, but the place she was taken wasn't a hospital. Aliens infused her with power from the star Betelgeuse, telling Catherine her new name was Stardancer, and that her mission was to make the Planet Earth a better place. The first time Stardancer flew, there was a song that was so beautiful Alyssa discovered that she was crying.

Rachel nudged her. "Hey. Are you okay?"

Alyssa wiped her eyes and nodded. "It's so pretty. It seems like I've heard it before."

47

"I haven't." Rachel took a long drink from her Coke.

Something swished the back of Alyssa's hair. A pale thing landed in Rachel's dark frizz. Popcorn. Alyssa picked it out. More popcorn pelted them.

Rachel turned to face Brooklynne and Mackenzie. "Why don't you guys grow up for a change?"

Alyssa heard their giggles. But Stardancer was still flying, and the song was too pretty to miss. "Remember your gift," the refrain continued. "Now let your light shine."

The scene shifted to a busy city street. A mother was having a hard time with her children. The two sisters were fighting. The older brother kept hiding, always checking to see if his mom would notice. The little brother walked quietly beside his mother. He had a blue helium balloon. A sleazy man was following the family. The balloon floated up, out of the little boy's hand. He yelled and chased after it, but he bumped into a parking meter and fell into the street just as a yellow taxi hurtled past. The mother screamed and dropped her purse as she ran to save her little boy. The bad guy grabbed the purse and the older brother. Other people were pointing and screaming. A shining figure meteored down from the sky. Stardancer pushed the taxi back with one booted foot. She picked up the mother and the little boy and set them safely on the sidewalk. Then she swooshed down on the escaping bad guy. Stardancer freed the boy and handed him his mother's purse, then lifted both of them and soared into the air. She dropped the bad guy in a rooftop swimming pool, and returned the boy to his mother. A shining light pulsed from her whole body.

Before she flew away, she knelt beside the children. "Make the world a better place," she told them. "Let your light shine."

The movie was so exciting that Alyssa actually forgot about Brooklynne and Mackenzie. She was disappointed that Allegra stayed the star of the dance academy — but maybe that was good in a way, because sometimes Stardancer had to leave in the middle of a performance. The song from the movie kept running through her head as she and Rachel went to the lobby afterwards. Parts of it were so familiar! But the movie was brand new, and so was the song. "I want to learn that song," she said to Rachel.

Rachel's mom was waiting. "Did you two have a good time?"

"Awesome!" Rachel said.

There was no more time to talk about the song. At Rachel's place they painted their fingernails and toenails with Rachel's new dark blue polish. Alyssa put Rachel's frizzy hair up like a dancer's — but it looked like a mop, instead, and Rachel collapsed on her bed, laughing. Alyssa got the giggles and couldn't stop. She rolled on the floor clutching her stomach. Rachel howled with laughter as she pretended to dust the furniture with her hair. The desk lamp fell over. When she dusted the dresser top, she misjudged distances and landed hard on the floor. "Ohhh!" she yelled. "Owww!"

Alyssa brought her a pillow. "The medic has arrived," she announced, "bearing a special cure from Betelgeuse...."

"Beetle juice?" Rachel yelped. "Yuk!"

There was a tap on the bedroom door. "Girls." Lori peeked into the room. "It's midnight. Time to settle down."

Rachel stood up. "Like my hair, Mom? If I dyed it blue, you could use it for a mop."

Lori laughed. "No thanks. I'd rather have my girl anytime." She gave Rachel a quick hug.

With the hug, a lonely feeling spiraled through Alyssa. How long had it been since Mom hugged her? It seemed like ages. But she wasn't going to wreck the good time by thinking about that. She dug in her backpack and pulled out the red pajamas that had been new at Christmas. When she stepped into the bottoms, blue toenails peered out from under the dark red legs. Rachel and Lori were still talking and laughing, so she slithered into her pajama top. Her fingernails looked *so* classy. She got her toothbrush from her backpack.

There, beside it, was the bubble envelope with the picture and the magnifying glass inside. Alyssa got them out. The best way to explain to Rachel would be with the picture itself. But — would Rachel believe her?

Rachel was telling Lori how Stardancer caught a school bus that a suicidal kidnapper had driven off a cliff. Alyssa smiled, remembering how she'd stopped that bus in midair as it hurtled toward jagged rocks and crashing waves. The pretty song came on again as Stardancer flew with the bus, and set it down safely in front of the school.

Humming the tune, Alyssa sat on the spare bed in Rachel's room. The magnifying glass slid out of the envelope, so she reached in for the picture too. The black-and-white photograph of the Clayton family looked out of place on the green-and-blue comforter. The faces of the Clayton family — her relatives? — looked up at her.

The girl, Deborah, seemed to smile. Rachel would think she looked like a nice person. Alyssa's heart beat faster. She didn't *have* to tell Rachel. She could just say these were the relatives for her project. For her project about Iowa Quakers and the Underground Railroad, she reminded herself. It still made her feel funny. But since Mom was like a zombie, was it really wrong to make a few things up? *It's lying,* a little voice said inside her.

She stared at Deborah's face in the picture. It almost seemed like Deborah was trying to say something.

Rachel and her mom had gone to the kitchen to make hot chocolate.

Alyssa stretched out on the bed. She could show Rachel the picture in the morning. For something to do, she held the magnifying glass so she could see Deborah's face up close.

Chapter Six

A horrible tingly feeling wrapped around her like a giant spider web.

Not now! Alyssa tried to drop the magnifying glass. Her muscles wouldn't obey. "Ra …" she started to scream, but suddenly it was hard just to breathe. Rachel's bedroom blurred, then swooped into dizzy blackness. Her head hurt. With a *bump* she slammed down.

"No," she moaned. At the same time, a heart-banging, breathless excitement gripped her. She tried to open her eyes and discovered that they already were open. Wherever she was, it was dark. Totally.

Bracing herself, Alyssa sat up. It felt like weeds were under her. "We should always try to notice things with all of our senses," Mrs. Fraser had said in class last fall, for a creative writing assignment. Funny how she could hear it now, like a recording in her brain.

Alyssa sat there in the dark. Hot, humid air surrounded her. Breezy gusts flapped her pajama legs. She stood up. "Rachel!" she yelled. "Get me back!" How did that work? Probably Rachel would think she was in the bathroom, or watching TV in the family room. What would they do when they couldn't find her? Mosquito bites pierced her cheek, her neck, and even through her pajamas. She slapped and felt a wet, squished insect on her jaw.

"Rachel!" she screamed again.

A dog started barking nearby. A rooster crowed.

Alyssa shivered. Was this the same place? What if it wasn't? What if somebody came out with a gun, and…?

A door banged not too far away. She turned and saw a gently swinging yellow light and, beside it, two legs. A dog bounded over to the person. "Is someone there?" a man's voice called.

Alyssa hung back. Anybody knew you didn't walk up to a strange man. *Especially* in the dark.

A white flare revealed dense clouds overhead. In that flicker of sight, Alyssa noticed trees and a weather vane on a barn. Thunder bowled across the sky. Chickens squawked. The dog whimpered as the sound died away.

"Sorry, old girl," the man said, petting the dog in the circle of light. "I know how badly these storms worry thee."

Alyssa's breath whooshed out in a relieved sigh. At least this man wouldn't be coming after her with a gun. Something squished between her bare toes. Mud, she hoped.

"It must've been some animal out in the pasture," the man continued. The light bobbed toward a building.

Lightning forked across the sky.

Wait! Alyssa wanted to yell. The thunder was louder this time. Again the chickens squawked and somewhere a horse whinnied. Wind lashed the treetops, hurling large drops of rain. The dog whined as the light swung its way to a screen door.

Alyssa drew in a sharp breath. "I'm here!" she said. The man didn't hear and went inside, but right away the dog barked and rocketed toward her. A deluge hissed down. She'd have to find cover.

The sky lit up. The dog was right in front of her now. It was the same black-and-white one she'd seen the other time the picture transported her.

The thunder blast came almost simultaneously. The dog huddled against Alyssa's legs, whining and stepping all over her bare feet with its rough pads and toenails. Almost instinctively her hand went down to comfort the frightened, wet animal. It sniffed at her palm, at her nail polish, at her pajama legs. Then it barked a sharp, decisive bark and pushed at her until she was forced to take a step in the direction of the house, then another and another.

Alyssa tried to hurry. Her foot landed on something soft with a nauseatingly-familiar smell. "Ewww," she said, hating her frustrated tears. She scraped her messy foot on the weeds or grass, whatever it was. Another flash of lightning showed that she stood at the edge of a huge garden.

The dog howled, an eerie sound that shot prickles across her skin. In the tumult of thunder and pounding rain, the yellow light appeared once more.

"Is there someone out here who needs help?" the man called.

"Yes!" Alyssa yelled.

This time the light came toward her — a lantern, she realized. "Let's get thee inside," the man said, helping her toward the house. "The folks on the radio said a fierce storm has swept through Redfield, so we're next."

The dog raced ahead and cowered on the front steps. Alyssa stumbled along, feeling small and foolish in her cold, clinging pajamas. Rain spattered into her face. The wind swept her hair across her eyes, across her mouth. Stinging marble-sized pellets whacked down, bouncing off the grass in the circle of lantern light.

"Hail." That one, terse word told Alyssa that this was terrible news.

A door squeaked open. Alyssa followed the man inside. The room smelled musty and was cluttered with boots and jackets. The dim glow of the lantern showed her other objects that she'd never seen before. The man pulled off his raincoat, hanging it on a hook on the wall, then discarded his wet shoes. He was wearing a long white shirt that came down to his knees and his legs were bare. Had he gotten out of bed when she screamed for Rachel? She felt bad, thinking about it — but also lucky.

"Here," he said, handing her a worn towel. "Thee will want to dry thyself." The rain on his wire-rimmed glasses reflected the lantern light.

Alyssa wiped her face and arms, but hesitated as she raised one muddy foot. "Go ahead." He nodded. After drying himself, he ushered her into another room.

Setting the lantern on a shelf, he lit a lamp with a wick, then turned a knob to extinguish the lantern.

She found herself in a large, old-fashioned kitchen. "Wait here," the man said quietly. "My wife will tend to thee." He pushed through a curtained doorway. Alyssa heard his footsteps thumping up creaky stairs.

Alyssa sat on a wooden chair. Except for the sound of the man's footsteps and a clock ticking somewhere, the house was intensely quiet. Outside, rain and hail slashed the windows; wind whipped through the trees and buffeted the walls. Thunder roared. Inside, it was hot and smelled faintly of cooking. The steady glow of the lamp revealed dishes stacked neatly on shelves, and matching tins of different sizes lined up on one counter. There was no fridge. No sink, either, except for a large washtub at one end of the counter with buckets beneath it. There weren't any water taps. In one corner sat a large, black boxy thing with a wide pipe rising from it. A calendar hung on the wall. Alyssa squinted at it in the dim light. According to the calendar, it was June. *June 1931!*

"Rachel," she whispered, and then said it louder. A knot swelled in her throat. Why did this have to happen? Rachel and her mom would be so scared when they couldn't find her.

At the sound of heavy footsteps, she looked up. Her first impression was of a football player in a housecoat, but really it was a pregnant woman. Her legs and arms were swollen, and her puffy face had a yellowish tinge. She looked as droopy as Mom, and sick.

"Oh my," the woman said, settling herself in a chair. "Thee's soaked right to the bone! Where did thee come from?"

Alyssa twisted her cold fingers together. "Um, North Dakota."

There was a flicker of recognition in the woman's tired eyes. "Would thee be the girl our Herbert found by the hen house not long ago?"

Relieved, Alyssa nodded. "I'm Alyssa Dixon." Lightning flared through the windows, followed by a bellow of thunder.

The woman clasped her hand and stared at her blue fingernails. "George," she called softly. "Bring a quilt, please. This girl is shivering. She'll need something of Deborah's to wear, too."

"Deborah?" Alyssa sat up straighter.

The woman smiled. "Our daughter's about thy age. You two look rather alike, in fact."

"Deborah *Clayton?*" she asked cautiously.

The woman looked startled. "Yes, we're the Claytons. My husband is George, and I'm Martha. How does thee know us? Did Herbert tell thee?"

Alyssa's teeth chattered. "It's kind of hard to explain." The stairs creaked as George Clayton came down with a quilt draped over one arm.

Gratefully she took it from him, but Martha stopped her before she had a chance to unfold it. "Thee won't get dry that way. First put on Debbie's nightgown."

Once the man had stepped out, Alyssa peeled off her wet pajamas, slipping into the blue flannel nightgown

Martha handed her. Definitely an improvement.

The woman shifted in her chair. "Our Debbie had quite the shock when thee vanished right before her eyes," she said. "What did thee do?"

Violent shivers seized Alyssa. She huddled into the quilt. "I don't know how. It's the picture ... a photograph."

"What does a photograph have to do with it?" George Clayton had returned to the doorway and was listening intently.

Alyssa squirmed, tucking her feet beneath her. "We have an old picture of relatives," she said. "The Clayton family — you guys, I think." Everything was sounding wrong. Thunder gave her a moment to think. "You're outside a house," she went on. "Four little kids are on a bench. Deborah and her big brother are standing beside you. I looked at it with a magnifying glass — looked at Deborah — and both times I ... came here."

"Oh my land!" Martha seemed to shudder. George Clayton stepped closer and squeezed her shoulders.

"Thee needs to be in bed, Martha," he said quietly. "Or we'll be calling the doctor out again. And thee, Alyssa — thee's no doubt feeling frightened and lost. Does thee know how to find thy way back home?"

"No." Tears spilled. She started sobbing and couldn't stop.

A warm hand rested on her shoulder. "Calm thyself, missy. Thee's far too old to blubber like that, and thee'll wake the others."

Startled, she looked up at him. "What?"

His gaze was firm but kind in the lamp light. "Thee heard."

"Sorry," she whispered. Thunder sounded in the distance.

Martha smiled. "We're glad to help. Thee's welcome to stay, Alyssa, as long as thee needs to."

Alyssa followed the adults up the steep stairs. The sky had begun to clear; the moon shone through the clouds. The girls' room was hot in spite of the open window. Moonlight revealed only one bed — with three distinct forms in it. The biggest girl had to be Deborah. As Alyssa stood there trying to decide where to put herself, Deborah's eyes opened and looked straight at her.

"Is thee the same girl who —?"

The whisper was so soft she had to scrunch down beside the bed to hear. "Yes. I was at my friend Rachel's, and ..."

"Shhh," Deborah cautioned. "We mustn't wake Eva and Frances."

There was an awkward pause. Alyssa wobbled in her crouching position.

"I couldn't help hearing," Deborah whispered. "I hoped it would be thee." She scooted closer to one of her sleeping sisters and patted the narrow empty space beside her. "I think thee'll fit."

Alyssa squeezed into the crowded bed. She'd never had to share before.

"Was the hail bad?" Deborah asked. "Mama and Daddy are so hoping for a good crop."

One of the little girls started snoring softly. "It hailed," Alyssa whispered back. "I don't know how bad it was."

There was a sigh, then a yawn. "Better sleep," Deborah said. "Morning chores come early, especially with Mama so sick."

A pang shot through Alyssa. Rachel didn't have the faintest idea where she was. Neither did Mom and Dad. And Mom was sick too, in a different way. She swallowed hard. Soon Deborah was breathing lightly, with her mouth open. It was a long time before Alyssa fell asleep.

Chapter Seven

The song from *Stardancer* was going through Alyssa's head when she woke up. "Remember your gift, now let your life shine," part of it had been. No — "let your *light* shine," not "life." Why couldn't she remember more of the words? The bed didn't feel right. Rachel didn't seem to be up yet, so she turned over drowsily for more sleep.

But the bed *really* didn't feel right. It was … wet. She sat up in a hurry. For a horrified moment she didn't know where she was.

"Thee's awake!" a small person said cheerfully, and crawled into her lap. Suddenly Alyssa's lap was wet too. The little girl looked up at her with big grey eyes. "Why are thy fingernails blue?" she asked. "And thy toenails too?"

Alyssa looked around the bedroom. It was a boxy room, and the ceiling slanted down on the side with the window. The walls were papered with wide, pale pink stripes. There was a chest of drawers against one wall, with a mirror on top, and near the door, a series of hooks holding girls' dresses of different sizes. Early morning sunlight shone into the room. Pink-checkered curtains hung in the window, fluttering slightly. Outside, a robin chirped.

"Thee! Alyssa!" The little girl patted her arm insistently. "Why are thy fingernails blue?"

"It's nail polish," she said. The girl, who was maybe four years old, didn't understand. "I painted them," she explained. "What's your name?"

"Frances." The girl snuggled against her, and the wetness spread. For an instant Alyssa felt like dumping her — but that would be mean. "Why'd thee paint thy fingernails?" Frances persisted.

"For fun." The cloying wetness and odour of urine were overwhelming, so she asked where the bathroom was. "We'll get you cleaned up," she said. That wasn't the only reason....

"A bath *room*?" The four-year-old didn't have any idea what she was talking about. "We have baths in the kitchen. On Seventh Day." Then she tugged at her nightgown. "I'm sorry I wet," she said.

It turned out that Deborah was the one who'd know what to do, since Mama had to stay in bed. And Deborah was doing chores. Alyssa took the hand that Frances offered. Together, they went down the creaky steps.

The kitchen was a busy place, but Deborah wasn't in it. A girl who was about seven stood on a chair by the black thing in the corner — a wood stove — stirring a pot of porridge. A little boy younger than Frances sat on the floor, stacking empty wooden spools. The boy Alyssa had met before — Herbert — tromped in carrying two buckets. Water sloshed over the rims as he set them by the large tub. "I see that Frances wet again," he said. He stared at Alyssa.

The girl at the stove turned around. Straight, light-brown hair bordered her freckled face. "Frances!" she said. "How could thee? If thee knew how much work it is to wash the sheets ..." Her glance fell on Alyssa, then her fingernails, and her brown eyes widened.

"Is there —?" Alyssa gestured helplessly. "I need to ... *go*." Her soaked red pajamas from last night were no longer on the kitchen floor; somebody had cleaned up after her. Shame burned in her face.

The girl understood. "The little house out back," she said.

Alyssa hurried down the path worn into the grass. The "little house" was unmistakable by its shape and the odour that hung in the air. In its dim interior, she saw two holes in a wide horizontal board. She sat down cautiously, feeling the cool wood against her skin. A fly buzzed lethargically in the early morning air. Then the door creaked open. Little Frances, still in her wet nightgown, climbed up to join her on the other seat.

Alyssa squeezed her eyes shut. She was supposed to be at Rachel's. What time was it there? Had they called Mom and Dad? The police?

There was no toilet paper. Ripped-off Sears catalogue pages sat in a wooden box nearby. After a moment, she knew what to do with them.

Frances followed her back up the path. "Eva's cross,"

she announced. "Mama's sick, and there's going to be a baby."

There was an irritable clucking. The rooster stepped forward, blocking their way. His reddish-brown feathers huffed out, and his angry red wattles swung as he looked at Alyssa with beady yellow eyes. She caught her breath and shrank backwards. This time she didn't have jeans on. Deborah's nightgown left her lower legs and bare feet exposed.

"Thee bad, wicked rooster!" Frances shouted. "I hate thee!" She clasped Alyssa's hand and pressed closer.

"Shoo!" Alyssa said, remembering what Herbert had done. But the rooster didn't move, and no broom was conveniently available. Instead, he advanced, flapping his wings. Alyssa edged sideways. The grass was still wet from the night's storm.

The rooster pursued them, clucking louder.

Frances whimpered. Still clinging to Alyssa's hand, she ducked behind her, leaving Alyssa face-to-face with the aggressive bird.

"Shoo!" she said, with rising panic.

The rooster flew at them. Frances shrieked. Stumbling backwards, Alyssa's bare foot tangled with a smaller one. She went down, trying to keep from landing on the little girl, at the same time hoping to protect her from the onslaught of pecks and scratches and the fierce, flapping wings.

An instant later she realized it was herself that she'd need to protect. She buried her face in the crook of her elbow, coughing in the feathery tumult. A raking scratch seared her forearm, then her scalp. There was a constant, high-pitched sound — Frances screaming?

For some reason she thought of Brooklynne, and how she'd taken the twenty dollars Dad gave her for groceries. She remembered the eggs splattering on the floor at Bristow's, and how Brooklynne had gloated while she searched her pockets for the money. That awful skit.... Tears smarted in Alyssa's eyes. Suddenly she was angrier than she'd ever remembered feeling before. Furiously, she hit out at the rooster. There was an irate squawk. Her hand closed around a scaly leg that reflexively pulled back. She hung on.

Abruptly, the rooster was off her. Its squawking rose to a frenzied pitch.

Blood oozed from a scratch on her forearm. Gasping, Alyssa sat up. Two long legs stood in front of her. Behind her, little Frances was sobbing. She looked up and saw Deborah's older brother standing there with a squirming bundle of feathers clamped tightly beneath his arm.

The boy looked at her, then at the wailing Frances, and again back at her. "This old man gave thee quite a beating," he said. He extended his free hand to help her up. "Is thee all right?"

"I don't know." Everywhere she thought about hurt, especially her scalp. Deborah's blue nightgown was splotched with mud. Angrily, she plucked a red-brown feather off her front. A curvy black tail feather lay beside the boy's foot, and she was glad. "Thank you," she added.

"Wilfred," Frances whined. "Carry me!"

Still clutching the rooster in its cramped, upside-down position, Wilfred lifted his little sister with his other arm. As she nestled against his chest, the wails subsided to choking gulps.

Wilfred headed up the path to the house, so Alyssa followed.

Deborah was in the kitchen, wearing an apron over the same dress she'd worn before. "Oh, Alyssa!" she said. "Thee looks awful!"

Alyssa chewed her lower lip to keep from crying. Everyone was staring.

Frances ran to her big sister and tugged at her flowered skirt. "Debbie! That wicked rooster bited me!" She pointed to her hand. Alyssa couldn't see any red marks anywhere on the little girl.

"Thee'll be fine," Deborah said, stroking Frances's hair.

With a pang, Alyssa remembered how Mom used to stroke *her* hair when she was upset. She looked down at the dirty hem of the nightgown and the drying mud on her bare feet. She didn't dare give in to the hurt. After all, she was too big to … *blubber*, George Clayton had called it. It made her think of whale fat. She looked away from Herbert's and Eva's staring eyes. The smallest boy — Charles — now was playing with something that looked like a corncob. And the calendar on the wall still said it was June 1931.

To avoid the intense scrutiny, she went to the black, boxy stove and stirred the thick porridge. She could hear the soft murmur and snaps as the flames devoured the wood, and smell the distinctive fragrance of wood smoke.

An instant later, Eva grabbed her arm. "Thee mustn't!" she said.

Alyssa pulled back, startled.

"Eva, thee could speak more pleasantly to our guest." Deborah's voice was stern.

"She'll get the mush dirty!" Eva's hair jiggled with her indignation. "I don't want to start all over."

Heat flooded Alyssa's face as she noticed the mud on her arms and hands, and the bits of outdoor debris on the sleeves of the nightgown. "I'm sorry," she mumbled. Couldn't she do anything right?

The door opened and Wilfred came inside with two buckets of milk. Alyssa watched as he poured it into a metal thing they called a "separator," then put a bucket beneath a spout at the bottom and began turning a crank. Deborah, having extricated herself from Frances, placed an empty can beneath a second spigot. Noticing Alyssa's stare, she explained: "We separate the cream. If we don't need it for butter, Daddy sells it in town." Thin, bluish milk trickled from the spigot at the bottom, while the yellowish cream dribbled into the can.

"Debbie, could thee finish?" Wilfred said. "There's another job —"

"I want to help!" Herbert's yell came through the open kitchen window.

Wilfred went back outside. A moment later, a chicken squawked.

"I'll take Mama her breakfast," Eva announced, and headed upstairs with a tray. There was a thud followed by a crash.

"Eva?" Martha called. "Is thee all right?"

Alyssa caught her breath. Eva was just a little girl, and those stairs were steep. It would be hard for a larger person to carry a tray up there. She glanced at Deborah. "I'll check on her," she offered.

Deborah shot her a grateful smile.

The tray had slid to the bottom of the stairs. Eva sat halfway up, beside a chipped bowl. Oatmeal and milk had spilled all over. Nearby were a spoon and the broken-off handle of a teacup. Eva's freckled face was flushed; her upper lip trembled, and then a tear raced down her cheek.

"Eva?" Martha's voice was sharp with worry.

"Everything spilled!" the little girl wailed. "That horrid loose board caught my foot and the tray tipped."

"She's okay," Alyssa called. When she sat down and put her arm around Eva's hunched shoulder, she was startled at the tension she found there.

Eva jerked away. "I don't want *thee*. I want Mama." Instead of running the rest of the way up the stairs, she buried her face in her hands, sobbing.

Alyssa picked up the bowl and spoon. The spilled porridge and milk were a mess, but there wasn't much she could do about it at the moment.

Eva's crying had a tight, desperate sound. "Why don't you go to your mom?" Alyssa said after an awkward pause.

"Daddy says we're not to worry her, on account of the baby," the little girl whimpered. There was a surprisingly loud hiccup.

Alyssa almost laughed. Just as quickly, a pang shot through her. They were worried about the unborn baby. Mom had never looked as sick and swollen as Martha Clayton. Was this baby going to die too? It was too awful to think about.

"Come, Eva," Martha said gently.

Alyssa extended her hand. A cold little hand clasped hers.

Martha's face was still puffy. "Is thee hurt, Eva?" she asked, beckoning them over to the bed. Her grey eyes acknowledged Alyssa, thanking her.

"I didn't mean to," Eva choked. She climbed up and nestled against her mother.

"Of course thee didn't, sweetheart."

Alyssa's throat ached at the tender way Martha cuddled Eva. Then Martha looked directly at her. "Is *thee* all right, Alyssa?" she asked. "What happened?"

"The rooster got me." It wasn't fair to divert attention away from the unhappy little girl. "I'll clean everything up," she added, and left the room.

Frances found her a rag. There was no running water. After filling a bowl from one of the buckets by the sink, she blotted the spilled milk and wiped up the oatmeal as best she could. Downstairs, a clock gonged seven. It seemed much later.

"Alyssa?" Deborah called. "I've heated water so thee can wash."

Only Deborah and little Charles were in the kitchen now. Deborah pulled a long curtain across one corner of the room, but even so, it was embarrassing taking off the blue nightgown, and just as embarrassing to see how dirty it was. Would the mud smears and grass stains wash out? Alyssa felt worse when Deborah didn't complain.

The hot, bracing water was sudsy thanks to a hard cake of soap. It felt wonderful on her face and neck, but the scratches on her arms and legs stung. "Thee looks more comfortable now," Deborah observed after she'd dried herself and squeezed into what turned out to be Deborah's second-best dress.

Comfortable wasn't exactly the word she would've chosen. It was strange looking down her front and seeing a rounded collar and little pink flowers on a skirt that reached below her knees. Her arms felt confined in the elbow-length sleeves. And the buttons.... She'd fumbled, straining to fasten them on the back of the dress, until Deborah did the job for her.

"Once Daddy and the boys are back, we'll have breakfast." Deborah sounded satisfied as she cut a loaf of homemade bread and set the individual slices on a cookie pan. "I'll take more mush up to Mama in a minute." She turned to Alyssa with a puzzled expression in her grey eyes. "Could thee tell me first, where thee's from? I don't understand at all!"

Chapter Eight

Alyssa gripped the back of a chair. One of the place mats on the table was crooked so she straightened it, as well as the silverware that had been laid out. "I don't know how to explain this," she said when Deborah's silence grew so long it was awkward. "I live in North Dakota."

"Yes." Deborah's grey eyes looked straight into hers. When she spoke next, she almost sounded impatient. "But thee's ... different. Thee simply *disappeared* into thin air! At first I thought I'd imagined thee, but Herbert and Wilfred and Daddy all saw thee, too. So did Flossie — and she simply barked, and *whined*, ever so much, when thee vanished. Thy clothes are different. And blue fingernails! Even with the town girls I've never seen that."

"Yeah." Alyssa wiggled her toes, looking at the startling colour. Rachel's bedroom, and the sleepover, seemed impossibly far away. "I think we're related," she said cautiously. "We have a picture of you guys."

Deborah began setting napkins around the table. "A picture? When was it taken?"

"1931." Last night, Martha and George had seemed upset when she mentioned it. A chill prickled Alyssa's arms. *There hadn't been a baby in the picture....*

"I live in ... the future," she said. "This will sound really weird, but every time I look at that picture, it's like you're smiling at me. And when I look at you with a magnifying glass, I come here. To this farm."

A napkin slipped from Deborah's hand. "Oh, my!" she said. "I never knew a person could do that!"

"Me neither." Alyssa picked up the napkin and put it on the table. "But things like that happen in some of the books I've read, and in movies."

Deborah's eyes shone. "What's it like? Can thee tell me?"

"I don't know if I can explain," she said. "I feel really dizzy. Kind of sick, actually. Everything gets dark — and then I bump down here."

"How strange," Deborah said. "How does thee get back home?"

"I don't know!" Alyssa said helplessly. "It only happened that one other time, and I landed on the couch. That's where I was sitting. I *think* it has something to do with the picture. But I don't know what."

Deborah clasped her hand. "Thee must feel frightened. I know I would."

Alyssa nodded, grateful for the warmth of Deborah's hand. For a minute neither of them spoke.

"There must be some reason this has happened," Deborah finally said. "Some purpose we can't understand." Then she gasped. "The mush! Eva will be upset if I let it burn." She hurried to the stove and stirred the oatmeal with a wooden spoon. "I'll take Mama some breakfast. Could thee make the toast? Just put it in the oven," she added, as Alyssa looked around for a toaster. "Then, if we hurry washing dishes, thee can come with me to the brook. I want to hear *everything* about thy world!" She gave Alyssa another one of her direct, searching looks. "I wonder — is thee a cousin? Or maybe my granddaughter?" She burst into giggles. "Imagine — me, a grandmother!"

Before Alyssa had a chance to reply that Grandma Hadley's name was Anne, Deborah put the slices of bread in the oven, then began assembling a second breakfast for her mother.

Frances wandered into the kitchen, carrying a large cloth doll. "This is Susannah," she said importantly. "My baby, and Eva's, and Debbie's baby. Does thee want to hold her?"

"Okay." For a moment, Alyssa felt silly reaching for the doll. It had been a long time since she'd played with dolls; all she had now was her ceramic horses. Susannah settled into her arms, looking up with twinkly black button eyes, a cute little nose, and a smiling mouth made with lots of careful stitches. Her hair was braided brown yarn that had been sewn onto her head. Somebody — was it Martha? — had spent a lot of time getting Susannah just right.

"Sing to Susannah," Frances commanded. "She's sad."

If anything, the doll looked relentlessly cheerful. Frances was gazing up at her expectantly. What to sing? "Erie Canal" or "Home on the Range?" "Hit the Road, Jack?" Definitely not "The Ants Go Marching" or "Battle Hymn of the Republic." The songs from school didn't seem right. Remembering the toast in the oven, she clasped the doll against her and peeked into the hot, dark interior. As far as she could tell, it still looked like bread.

"Sing!" Frances insisted.

Reluctantly, Alyssa hummed the first tune that came into her head. She couldn't remember most of the words. Where was the song from? When she got to "Remember your gift, now let your life shine," it came back to her — it was the *Stardancer* song, from last night. Alyssa sang the song again, searching for more words. "When times are dark, and (la-la-la-la) alone, (something, la-la-something) cast in stone. (Something-la-la-la) divine, remember your gift, now let your light shine." It was "light," not "life," the way she'd sung it first.

"That's not right," Frances said. "Songs don't have 'la-la-somethings!'"

For an instant Alyssa was tempted to throw the doll at her. But her arms felt settled around Susannah who, with her sewn-on face and hair, and her pink-checkered dress, must be about the same size as a real baby. Would Charlotte have been this size? How would it have felt, having a baby sister she could hold and hug? She swallowed hard and made herself sing again.

Frances jumped up and down. "Stop!" she said. "I told thee, thee can't just sing 'la-la-something.' That's not a song!"

Deborah was back. She picked up the struggling Frances with obvious effort. "Thee mustn't be rude, Frances. It's a pretty tune, and if Alyssa doesn't know all the words, we'll make up some that fit."

Frances swung her dangling feet and glowered. "'Something-something-la' is wrong. Susannah wants a *real* song."

Alyssa almost put the doll on the set table, but moved her to one of the chairs as Herbert, Wilfred, and George came in. There was starting to be a smell of burning toast. She glanced at Deborah, but Herbert had pushed his way between them.

"What a chase!" Herbert's eyes glinted. "I thought we'd never get him!" His freckled face was cleaner than it had been earlier, and his hands and arms shone wetly. Dark-red spots were scattered across his blue overalls.

"Not now," Wilfred said. "Thee'll upset our guest."

"The toast —" Alyssa gestured helplessly toward the stove.

But Frances was wriggling down from Deborah's arms. She ran to Wilfred instead. "Pick me up!" she insisted. "That horrid, wicked rooster bited me." Then she squealed with laughter as her biggest brother swooped her up almost to the ceiling.

"He can't peck thee now," Herbert announced smugly.

Deborah shot Alyssa a knowing look. "I'll get Eva," she said.

Wisps of smoke leaked through the cracks around the oven door.

"'Moke! 'Moke!" little Charles cried, pointing.

"Who's in charge of the toast?" Wilfred asked.

Helplessly, Alyssa looked around for oven mitts. Nothing — no oven mitts, nothing recognizable as a pot-holder. Grabbing a dish towel, she opened the heavy oven door. Choking smoke billowed into her face.

"Pee-*yew*!" Herbert said.

The dish towel was too thin, and searing pain lanced her hand. Alyssa sagged onto her knees, trying to keep the blackened toast from sliding onto the floor, but several slices skittered away. Tears blurred her vision. She sat there on the wooden floor, protecting her burned hand against her middle.

"I'll help thee," said a quiet voice. Wilfred knelt beside her, gathering up the evidence of the disaster.

The fiery pain didn't ease up. Looking at her hand, Alyssa saw angry blisters forming on her fingertips and on the webbing between her hand and thumb. She sniffled and pressed her trembling lips together. "Is there any more bread?" she asked.

"Never mind," Wilfred said. "This will scrape off. Herbert!" he ordered. "Scrape the toast. Alyssa's burnt her hand."

Herbert looked at her hand. "Ow," he said sympathetically. "Thee needs some butter on that. That's what Mama always says."

Butter? An ice cube was more like it — and Vitamin E, or maybe aloe plant goo. Why couldn't she be at home, where people knew what to do, and everything wasn't so *hard*? Alyssa gave in to the tears, shuddering as somebody smeared greasy butter on all the places that hurt. Friendly hands guided her to a chair at the table. "Where's Susannah?" Frances's piercing voice hurt her head. Then, a shriek, accompanied by the sound of small, stomping feet: "Herbert! Don't sit on Susannah!"

"Just *shut up!*" Luckily no one seemed to hear her, in the noise. Her teeth clenched. "Can't thee ever —" Realizing what she'd just said, Alyssa squeezed her eyes shut, trying to tune everything out.

Breakfast started in a way that was eerily familiar — everyone holding hands for a silent grace. Deborah thoughtfully didn't clasp Alyssa's burned hand. After that it was an overload of newness with so many people eating at once, and food that was nothing like the granola, dry cereal, or waffles Alyssa was accustomed to. And a greasy hand that hurt too much to hold a spoon comfortably. Alyssa squeezed her elbows close to her sides, surrounded by moving arms and chattering voices. The milk was warm — straight from a cow, she realized. Then everybody was done, and she was still nibbling at her burned toast, and her hand still hurt. The homemade apple preserve was tasty, but not the sort of thing she usually had with toast. Behind her, somebody started scraping dishes.

The bigger boys trooped outside with their father. Deborah was talking to Eva about needing boiling water. Little Charles scooted past, rolling an empty wooden spool. "Susannah, Susannah, Susannah," Frances crooned in a shrill, lilting voice. Alyssa rested her tired head on the table and wished she were home. No dizzy spell conveniently whisked her away.

"Alyssa." Deborah's hand touched her shoulder. "Could thee please hold the door open? Eva and I have to carry this pot outside."

Feeling guilty, she looked up. A huge steaming pot sat on the stove. It was so big.... How could Eva and Deborah possibly manage it? "I'll help carry it," she said, standing up.

"No," Deborah insisted. "Thy hand's already hurt, and thee can't afford another accident. Just hold the door."

Another accident? Was that how they all thought about her? Alyssa bit her lip hard and did what she'd been asked. Outside, the two other girls set the heavy pot on a low weather-beaten table.

Flossie came running to greet them. She had something in her mouth. Before Alyssa had a chance to see what it was, the dog looped around to sniff at Herbert — or, rather, what he was carrying. Herbert strode over and dumped a bundle that looked like brownish feathers into the steaming pot. A soggy, musty smell rose into the air. "Look at him now!" Herbert said triumphantly. "Mean old thing finally got what he deserved." He made a hacking sound.

Deborah sighed and began prodding at the thing with a stick.

A yellow claw lay on the grass. In the pot, a curved black feather rose to the surface. Alyssa's stomach lurched.

Herbert staggered around, laughing. "Rooster stew!" he hooted. "Tough old rooster stew!"

"Here, Flossie," Eva called.

The black-and-white dog came obligingly. But when Eva reached out to her, Flossie snarled and backed off, tail still wagging. Whatever she had in her mouth was terribly important to her. "Thee's horrid," Eva said.

Something red dangled from the side of the dog's mouth. As Alyssa watched, it slid onto the grass. Flossie put her foot on top of it, guarding her prize — but not before Alyssa had seen the chewed, now-eyeless brown head of the rooster, with its yellow beak and red, bloody wattles.

Dizzying nausea roared through her. Alyssa sagged forward and vomited into blackness.

There was a collision. A shriek. And a soft surface.

Humiliated, Alyssa wiped her mouth, too late remembering the burns on her hand. Something — butter, she remembered — smeared across her cheek. In her lap — in her *skirt* — was a mess containing unmistakable bits of burned toast and oatmeal.

"Alyssa! Where *were* you?"

It was Rachel. She was back on the bed in Rachel's room, where she'd been when she looked at the photograph.

A convulsive sob wracked her. "Rachel," she wailed. "I'm sorry! This mess ... How can I ever tell thee what —"

"I'll get Mom," Rachel interrupted. "She is completely, *absolutely*, freaked." She headed for the door. "What do you mean, 'ever tell the what?'"

The vomit had soaked through the front of Deborah's dress. Alyssa shuddered. "How can I ever *tell* thee ... oh ..." She was saying "thee" again.

Rachel crinkled her nose. "The ... secret? The ... answer? Finish your sentence!" It was obvious that she'd been crying.

"Tell *you*." Alyssa wiped her unhurt hand on the folds of the skirt. Poor Deborah; this was her second-best dress. Would she ever get it back?

Rachel stood there impatiently. "Where'd you get that dress?" she asked. "What happened to your pajamas? Where did you *go*?"

"The picture!" Panicked, Alyssa fumbled for it. If she'd barfed on the picture ... Thank goodness — it was facing down.

Lori appeared in the doorway. "Alyssa, honey!" She crossed the room and gathered Alyssa into a hug, dress, vomit, and all. "We've been terrified."

Alyssa sagged against Lori. It felt so good to be hugged. "I'm so sorry," she said. "It's hard to explain."

"It's three in the morning," Rachel said. "Your dad's looking for you."

Three in the morning? Alyssa felt cold all over.

"We'll call his cell and let him know you're safe." Lori straightened up. "Alyssa, honey, let's get you cleaned up. Where'd the dress come from?"

"Iowa," she said numbly. "From one of my old relatives."

But Rachel and her mother weren't listening. Lori got the cordless phone. "Greg," she said, "she's here. She's safe." A minute later, Alyssa was in the bathroom, where

Lori started hot water running and lathered a washcloth. "You'll feel much better once you're cleaned up," Lori murmured. "Rachel, hon, go get Alyssa's clothes."

Alyssa gasped when the washcloth rubbed the burns on her hand. Lori noticed. "Alyssa, what happened to your hand? Whoever snuck in and took you — what did those people do to you?"

Lori and Rachel must think she'd been kidnapped. "It's not like that!" she said.

The doorbell rang.

Chapter Nine

"Quick," said Lori. "Let's get you dressed. Rachel, go see who's at the door. Don't open it unless it's Greg."

Alyssa jammed her legs into her jeans, then yanked her sweatshirt over her head. She brushed her teeth, thankful for the cool, minty taste. How was she ever going to explain to Dad?

He was in the living room, sagged on the couch. Alyssa couldn't remember ever seeing him so tired — except on that awful day, after what happened at the hospital. He stood up slowly. "Lyssa! Are you all right?"

She nodded, and was enfolded in a trembling hug.

"What happened to you?" Dad's voice was croaky.

Alyssa pulled back. "I ..." She'd never been any good at fibbing; no matter what she said, nobody would believe her. "I was in Iowa," she mumbled.

"*What?*" Three shocked faces stared at her.

"In the past," she stammered. "Old relatives, the Claytons —"

But they'd quit listening. Voices rose. She was bundled into the minivan, where she clutched her backpack to her chest. Her hand still hurt. As the familiar streets swooshed by, there were no other vehicles. She and Dad seemed trapped in a silence that was too big to penetrate.

The lights were on at home. It looked weird, next to the neighbours' dark houses. Alyssa noticed that the house key clattered against the doorknob before Dad managed to unlock.

"They're here," Ethan yelled the minute Alyssa followed Dad inside. He was waiting by the door, wearing a t-shirt and his boxers. "Where'd you go?" he asked.

Alyssa didn't answer because it seemed pointless. Ethan's eyebrows looked like Wilfred's — and Eva's, the longer she thought about it.

There was a swish of clothing in the hallway. "Alyssa?" Mom appeared. As always, her hair was a greasy mess. For an instant Alyssa could see Martha Clayton's face — and how, even though she'd been in bed, her hair was neatly parted and brushed. Then she was enfolded in a hug that smelled of unwashed skin and dirty clothes. Alyssa held her breath.

Nearby, she could hear Dad yawning. "After all that searching," he said, "she says she was in Iowa." He sighed loudly. "I guess we'll get the truth out of her tomorrow."

Eyes stinging, Alyssa yanked away from her smelly mother and ran down the hall to the bathroom. The mirror showed her a red, angry face and tangled hair. There was even something caught in it — a tiny rust-coloured feather. And she'd gone around looking like *that?* Alyssa inspected the burn blisters and the rooster scratches on her arms. She fumbled in the medicine cabinet for the Vitamin E ointment. Then she sat on the toilet and cried.

After a while Ethan's characteristic knock sounded on the door. "Are you still in there?" he asked.

Alyssa wiped her eyes and flushed. "I'm making hot chocolate," he whispered as she came out. "Come to the kitchen if you want some."

Hot chocolate? That was how she'd happened to look at the picture in the first place. The clock on the microwave said it was 4:12. But she wasn't sleepy, because she'd already slept — in 1931.

Ethan poured milk into two mugs and set them in the microwave. "You said you were in Iowa?" he whispered.

She'd never thought about telling Ethan. Except for Mom, it might make the most sense to him. "Yes," she said cautiously. "It happened once before. I never told anybody."

"Huh?"

"It *did*!" Alyssa got her backpack and dug in it for the photograph. "It's this picture," she said. "When I look at Deborah Clayton — the oldest girl — with the magnifying glass, I ... go there." She looked at the old black-and-white photograph. Something was different. Flossie! The dog hadn't been in the picture before, but now she sat by Herbert's legs, grinning at the camera. And ... wasn't Deborah wearing a different dress? She thought about the dress that Lori had promised to wash, and shivered. "Weird! It changed!" Her hand shook as she gave the photo to her brother.

Ethan studied the picture. The microwave beeped.

"I'll do the hot chocolate." Alyssa stirred the chocolate powder into the mugs and took a swallow. Warm and creamy, it relaxed something inside her.

Ethan took the other mug and gave her a scrutinizing look. "Think it'd work for me?" he said.

Startled, Alyssa slopped hot chocolate down her chin. "You believe me?" Marigold appeared and rubbed against her legs.

Ethan shrugged. "If nothing happens, I'll know you made it up. Or were hypnotized, or something. How'd you get back?"

"I have no idea." Alyssa bent over to pet the cat. "If you disappear too, maybe they won't think I'm lying." Something inside her jealously hoped that it wouldn't work for Ethan.

Standing there in his underwear, with his shaggy hair falling into his eyes, her brother looked more closely at the photograph. "It's like that girl Deborah's staring right at me," he said after a moment.

Alyssa's heart started beating hard and fast. "Ethan ..."

He set his hot chocolate on the counter. "Gimme the magnifying glass."

Down the hall, a bedroom door opened. Dad's footsteps thumped toward the kitchen. "What are you two doing?" he demanded.

"I can't sleep," Alyssa said.

At the same time, she heard Ethan's mumbled, "It's Saturday now, so who cares?"

Dad gave an exasperated sigh. "You may not care, but I have a class to teach in about six hours." Like Ethan, he, too, was in his underwear and socks. Dark stubble covered his jaw and chin.

As if he'd noticed her stare, Dad looked straight at her. "Iowa," he muttered. "Why on earth would you imagine going there? Why not Disneyland, or Hawaii? Or even Alaska?"

Something flickered across Ethan's face. "What's wrong with Iowa?" For whatever reason, he was challenging Dad. Alyssa looked at him, then at their father. Tension seemed to quiver between the two of them.

"Maybe I want to find out more about my ancestors," Alyssa said. "For my genealogy report." Right away she hated how she'd said it. Dad had been really scared, driving around looking for her at three in the morning.

Dad drew in a sharp breath. His mouth tightened. "Kids!" he muttered as he went down the hall.

Ethan rolled his eyes eloquently. "Where's the magnifying glass?" he whispered.

"Not in here," Alyssa whispered back. "When you land, you ... crash."

"Let's go to my room. That way the Male Parent won't make such a stink." Without waiting for her to answer, Ethan headed down the basement stairs. Marigold darted after him. Alyssa gulped the last of her hot chocolate and slung her backpack over her shoulder.

The computer was on in Ethan's room; a red screensaver glided serenely across the dark monitor. Alyssa stood in the doorway while her brother kicked aside heaps of clothes on the floor. She noticed that the sole was almost completely off one of his shoes.

She nudged it with her foot. "Haven't Mom or Dad noticed?" she said.

Ethan's mouth tightened in a way that looked uncannily like Dad's. "Why would they?" There was a bitter twist in his voice.

For an instant she felt like hugging her brother — tall, gangly, and looking suddenly vulnerable in his t-shirt and boxer shorts.

Ethan flopped onto his rumpled bed and studied the picture of the Claytons. "Have you got the magnifying glass?"

Alyssa handed it to him. Ethan brushed hair out of his eyes, then held the lens steady over the photo. "It's like she's smiling at me," he said.

The air in the room seemed to shudder. Goosebumps shot down Alyssa's arms and legs. Her neck prickled. On the floor, Marigold growled a low, eerie cat growl. His fur puffed out; then he hissed and ran from the room.

"Huh?" Ethan looked at the empty doorway. He yawned hugely. "Oh well," he said, and stretched out on his bed. The magnifying glass slid onto the floor. The photograph of the Claytons lay on the pillow near Ethan's head.

"Ethan?" When he didn't move, Alyssa called his name again, louder. Was he all right? Was this what had happened to her? Except ... Rachel and Lori hadn't been able to find her. *At all*. And she'd come back wearing Deborah's dress. The burns and the scratches proved that her physical body had been someplace else. How else could she have gotten that rooster feather in her hair? She touched Ethan's shoulder.

He squirmed away. "Lemme sleep," he mumbled.

Sleep? Something bizarre had happened with the picture. She'd felt the air change — and Marigold reacted to it.

"Ethan!" she said again.

He rolled over. His breathing settled into a soft, drowsy rhythm.

Should she leave him like that? Alyssa sat down at the computer and keyed her password into the messaging system. When the box opened, she typed:

> rache — 2 weird, i don't get it. ethan
> looked at the picture using the magni-
> fying glass. now he's — sleeping??? was
> i gone? u couldn't find me, right? have
> 2 talk 2 u asap.

It was awkward doing everything with her left hand because of her burns. Would Rachel understand? Had she even mentioned the photo of the Claytons? Probably not.

The clock on the computer said it was 4:49. Alyssa leaned back in the chair and clicked to a search engine. She keyed in "Iowa." Confronted with page after page of blue links, she backtracked and typed in "Stardancer." One site had the song and clips from the movie.

After a while she looked over at Ethan. He was still asleep. The picture of the Claytons had moved. It seemed in danger of falling between the bed and the wall. Holding her breath, she reached across her brother.

As her fingers touched the print, the air pressure seemed to change.

Ethan stirred. Then he sat up in a hurry. "What are you doing in here?" he mumbled.

Chapter Ten

"What happened?" Alyssa demanded. "Tell me!"

Ethan looked drowsy and disoriented. "What do you mean, 'What happened?' You woke me up, is what happened."

"But —" Alyssa held the picture in front of him. "Don't you remember? You were looking at this. You wanted to …" Was there any point explaining if he didn't remember?

"Huh?" Ethan was slightly pale; his freckles looked like scattered cinnamon. Just like Herbert's and Eva's. She shivered. It would be amazing if she could have a picture of the three of them together. And of Deborah and herself! Everybody said they looked so much alike.

"Were you having any dreams?" she asked.

Ethan rubbed his eyes. "Why's it such a big deal? I was only sleeping." He squinted at the clock. "It's five in the morning — why wouldn't I be asleep?"

Alyssa sighed and put the picture back in the padded envelope.

Across the room, the computer dinged, while the red screensaver kept spilling itself across the dark screen.

Ethan got up and clicked the mouse. "What were you doing in my message box?"

"I was in my message box, not yours." As he started typing, she wished she could shake her brother. "*Something* happened," she insisted. "Remember how the air changed and Marigold freaked?"

Uncertainty flickered in Ethan's face. "Are you sure?" His fingers kept typing.

"Yes!"

Again the computer dinged. Ethan leaned forward. "Cripes," he muttered. "Denmark's going to the playoffs?"

"Ethan. Alyssa to planet Ethan."

"Shh. I'm busy."

Alyssa stamped her foot. "Ethan. Just tell me what happened. *Please?* I'm supposed to be at Rachel's right now. At the sleepover, remember?"

"So?"

Alyssa gritted her teeth. "You're so in love with that computer. Nothing else matters."

Ethan shrugged.

On the floor by his desk, the power bar switch glowed like a little red eye. She nudged it with her toes; at an irresistible impulse, she pressed it. There was a satisfying click and the screen went blank. Ethan yelled.

Heavy footsteps sounded above them.

"Now look what you did," Ethan said.

"You yelled, not me!" But it was too late; Dad had already tromped in.

His face was a dull brick colour. "Your mother and I are trying to sleep." Each word was a small explosion.

Alyssa cringed. "I'm sorry," she mumbled.

"*You* made all that noise?" Dad looked at her in surprise.

"I did." Ethan stood up and stared right at Dad. Alyssa noticed that he was almost as tall as their father. "And I apologize for waking you up."

Dad glared right back. "I would hope so. Get to bed. *Now*. Both of you."

Alyssa dropped the padded envelope safely into her backpack and scuttled up the basement stairs. "... Turn ... computer off!" Dad's voice followed her. "... Last I knew, I'm paying ... bills ... *Alyssa!*" She froze at his yell. "Not so fast. You're grounded until further notice."

Grounded? As she stumbled past the baby's room on the way to her bedroom, Alyssa clutched the backpack against her. It would serve them right if she disappeared forever. She could do it too and nobody would know what happened. Except Ethan, maybe. And who'd believe him?

She crawled into bed without changing. Would Mom notice her missing pajamas? Probably not. But if Mom got on her case about it ... well she'd just have to go back to Iowa to get them.

The green LED numbers on her clock radio said 5:37. She heard the gentle thump of the newspaper being placed in the mailbox. It wasn't long ago that Ethan had been doing their paper route. She shuddered, thinking of the little photograph of Charlotte's lifeless face — and thinking of Martha Clayton, who'd looked so sick and bloated. After Charlotte, Ethan sometimes didn't get up in time, and people complained. And then he quit, just like that.

She pulled her covers up to her chin. Ethan was so different, now. Standing up to Dad. And — why'd he have to brush her off like that? As if some sports playoff was more important! In a surge of frustration she flung her pillow toward her closet. There was a thud. A cat yowl. Marigold fled from her room; his feet were tangled in something. Alyssa lay there and couldn't sleep.

The next morning she had a sore throat and gritty eyes. Except for a dream about lying in bed while the rooster walked all over her, she was positive she hadn't slept at all.

When Dad called her out to the kitchen, Mom was actually at the table for once. Alyssa poured herself a bowl of wheat squares. Sitting there — while Ethan slept in — she wished she were at Rachel's place.

Instead, Dad was interrogating her. "Alyssa," he said. "Let's hear what happened last night. You say that nobody abducted you. So why did you leave Rachel's house? Do you have even the faintest idea how worried everyone was? We were on the verge of calling the police."

"Honest! I never —" Helplessly, Alyssa looked to Mom, who sat there stirring her coffee. *Clink, clink, clink* — the spoon kept circling, hitting the sides of the mug. Alyssa clenched her teeth. "Quit it!" she muttered under her breath.

"Then how do you explain your absence?" Dad persisted. "Lori Lowell was frantic. Did she and Rachel go out for a while and leave you there alone?"

How could Dad think that about Lori? These days, Rachel's mom paid more attention to her than her own parents did. Agreeing with Dad would get her off the hook, but how could she tell that kind of lie about her best friend? Alyssa jammed some dry cereal into her mouth to put off answering.

Dad waited for a moment. When she didn't answer, he said, "I see. I guess we'll have to have a talk with the Lowells."

"No!" It came out in a splatter of food. Alyssa wiped her mouth. "It wasn't them. I *told* you, I looked at a picture of the Claytons — and suddenly I was in Iowa. By accident." There was no point in adding the part about 1931.

Mom's clinking hesitated. Dad gave Mom a sour look. "Say something, Jennifer," he said. "Do you accept Alyssa's explanation? It's about time you took some responsibility for our children."

The spoon clanked against the side of the mug and stood there. Mom's dirty hair dangled in her face. There was a heavy silence.

Alyssa's stomach twisted. She felt like dumping her uneaten cereal on the table, and spilling her milk and juice. Would Mom notice *that?*

Mom started smoothing her paper napkin. Her hands looked naked without her wedding ring. She'd taken it off when her hands got swollen, when she was pregnant. Did it bother Dad that she wasn't wearing it now? Mom's mouth trembled. "You don't know what it's like."

Dad sighed. "Leave everything to me. Like always. Alyssa, just tell us …"

After a while it was more than Alyssa could take. "You're just asking me to make something up!" she yelled. "To tell a complete fib." She extended her arms; orange marmalade on one of the plastic mats globbed onto her elbow. "Look." She pointed to the scratches. "That's where the rooster got me. And see?" She shoved her blistered hand in front of her parents. "That's from when I took the burnt toast out of the oven." Mom drew in a sharp breath. So — even with all that fuss, nobody had gone to the trouble of actually looking at her.

The phone rang. Alyssa lurched to get it, but Dad was closer. "I'm sorry, Rachel," he said after a moment. "Alyssa can't talk right now. She's having some quiet time at home." There was a pause. "She'll phone you in a few days."

"That's not fair!"

But Dad was still on the phone. "Ethan?" he said. "As far as I know, he's asleep in his room."

Heat flooded her face, even her ears. Rachel had received her message and was calling back—just like she'd asked. "Let me talk to her! Please?"

But Dad had already hung up.

Something made her remember how Mrs. Fraser asked them to role-play strong emotions. Tristan and Kai were wrong. "Murderous rage" wasn't about pretending to stab people. There was a kind of exploding meanness inside that made her feel like throwing poison in Dad's face. And maybe poking him with something burning hot. He'd look surprised, and then ...

She couldn't imagine Deborah *ever* wanting to do something like that. But Herbert had been happy about the rooster. Tears slid down her cheeks. Again. George Clayton had said, "Thee's too big to blubber."

Mom looked up at her. "What picture are you talking about, Alyssa?" she asked. "Your Great-Grandmother Newlin was a Clayton."

"I'll get it!" Alyssa ran down the hall to her room.

Her bright blue backpack wasn't on the floor, not even buried under dirty clothes. Her closet? She couldn't remember putting it there, but she'd been so frustrated she might've done it without thinking. No luck. She couldn't see it under her bed. Alyssa's heart pounded harder. Had Ethan taken it?

She ran down the basement stairs. Her brother was sprawled across his bed, the covers halfway up his chest, and he was snoring with a faint, whispery sound. There was no sign of her backpack.

Upstairs, Mom would still be sitting there in her nightgown and dirty bathrobe. Probably Dad was tapping his fingers impatiently; pretty soon he had to teach his Saturday class. Maybe he'd tap the smeared butter and marmalade where his knife had fallen off his plate.

Her parents were exactly as she'd imagined them. Except the butter smear had been cleaned up. She hoped Dad got it all over his arm.

"I can't find it!" she said. And suddenly, she knew exactly what "despair" felt like.

Ethan was still asleep when Dad left to teach. Alyssa banged the leftover breakfast things onto the kitchen counter, not caring when silverware clattered across the floor. She slammed the empty cereal bowls into the sink and felt a mutinous satisfaction when a big chip split off one of them. Then she remembered a bowl of oatmeal dropped on steep stairs, and a teacup with its handle broken. She stood there, shaken. "Mom?" she called.

"Just a minute." Her mother's muffled voice came from the living room. "I found some pictures of Great-Grandmother Newlin's family."

"Really? Let me see!" Alyssa barged into the living room. Mom was sitting on the couch with a few photos spread out in front of her on the cluttered coffee table. She flopped down beside her mother and looked at one black-and-white photo, then another, with a growing disappointment. "These are too old," Alyssa said. She considered going to her room — but Mom had actually paid attention to what she'd said, and even went to the trouble of finding these pictures. "Thanks, Mom," she said. It came out sounding icky-polite, in a sucking-up kind of way. Mom would know they weren't what she wanted.

Mom was too quiet. Alyssa had the sudden feeling that she'd better keep talking. "Maybe I can write about these people for my report," she said. She looked at the back of one of the photos. 1914. Only a few were

Claytons, and nobody looked familiar. There were Goodens and Standings, and Hocketts and Cooks. The oldest men and women sat on benches; those men all had bushy beards. Gathered around them were families with children of different ages. Alyssa squinted as she studied the faces. Should she tell Mom more about what happened?

Her mother straightened unexpectedly. "There's an album somewhere. I could look for it."

"No —" Alyssa caught her mother's sleeve. *Don't leave me!* she almost said. But that was wrong; *she,* not Mom, was the one who'd been missing. Mom was just ... gone from being her usual self. *Ask questions,* something inside her prompted. "Um ... Do you know of George and Martha Clayton?"

"They're your ..." Mom counted on her fingers. "Your great-great grandparents. Their ancestors came over from England sometime in the 1800s." Mom looked straight at her, then at her burned hand. "That must really hurt," she said, reaching and carefully not touching the reddened places. "What have you put on it?"

Alyssa chewed her lip. "Butter," she mumbled. "They put butter on it. And when I got home, I put on some Vitamin E."

"Maybe we should take you to the clinic." Again Mom held her eyes. "Is there anything else I need to know? That a doctor should know?"

"What?" Puzzled, Alyssa looked at her blistered burns, and at her scratched arms. "It doesn't hurt all the time. Not anymore."

Mom fidgeted with a pile of papers on the coffee table. "That's not what I meant, Alyssa."

"The Claytons were really nice to me," she said in a rush. Didn't Mom understand? After all, one of the Clayton sisters was Mom's grandma!

"Alyssa." Mom's voice was very tense. Suddenly Alyssa didn't want to look at her. "Were you molested?"

"*What?*" Alyssa jumped to her feet. Photographs slid to the floor. "The Claytons? They're nicer than —"

Mom sagged back on the couch.

It seemed like a poisonous grey cloud settled in the living room, filling up every particle of space. Alyssa's eyes stung. "And now you won't even let me see Rachel," she shouted. "It's not fair!" When she took a step to leave, her foot slid on something.

It was two pictures. Something in her felt like ripping them into tiny pieces and throwing them at Mom. But if they were the Claytons …

Alyssa sat sideways in the reclining chair so she wouldn't have to see Mom. One picture was of an older teenager. She had clear eyes and she was smiling. Something about her was familiar — but it wasn't Deborah. Holding her breath, Alyssa looked at the back. *1915*, the inscription read. *Martha Gooden*. Suddenly she knew, without any doubt. This was Martha Clayton! Alyssa's hands shook as she looked at the last photo.

They were outside their house. The date on the back was 1926. George and Martha were seated on chairs, and standing beside them were a much-younger Wilfred and Deborah, who was probably about six. The little boy in George's lap had to be Herbert. Martha was holding a child too, a toddler who had Eva's serious expression.

But there was another girl in the picture. She was smiling right at the camera, and she and Deborah were holding hands. Deborah was a little bit taller, so they probably weren't twins. Alyssa's breath caught. Her skin prickled, especially at the roots of her hair. Was it *her*? It almost looked like her class picture from kindergarten. But that was impossible. She turned the picture over to read the back. There were their names: *George and Martha Clayton. Wilfred, George, Herbert, Martha, Eva, Deborah, Bertha.*

Bertha Clayton? There was no Bertha in the 1931 picture. And nobody had said anything about a Bertha. That must mean …

Alyssa's throat clenched. She looked over at her mother, on the couch, with her dirty hair and clothes. "Can't you even take a bath?" she screamed. Holding the pictures, she ran out of the living room.

Chapter Eleven

Rachel and her mother didn't come to Quaker meeting the next morning. Mom came, though. Emptiness filled Alyssa as she sat in the quiet room, looking at chairs where Rachel might have sat. Were Rachel and Lori mad? Did they think she ran away? Or had Dad said something that upset them?

Warren Stanley's face looked peaceful as he sat there with his eyes closed. The sun coming through the window shone on his white hair. When Alyssa shut her eyes halfway, his head seemed to be shining, like a light.

She wiggled in her squeaky chair. Mom looked at her. Not with a frown or a smile, but at least she looked. Her hair wasn't dirty! Alyssa had been sure something was different at breakfast, but in the busyness of getting ready to go, she hadn't paid much attention.

One of the newer women started talking about the war — how whole families were homeless, with relatives killed or missing because of the bombing. This lady often spoke in meeting for worship, and sometimes she cried. *Don't cry!* Alyssa thought, over and over. It was too embarrassing when grownups got weepy. At last the talking stopped. Alyssa sighed and felt the silence set-tling through the room again.

Was there going to be another peace march? That made her think of Rachel. Alyssa stared at the calendar by the photocopier. Now it showed a picture of a red farm machine.

There was too much to think about. Rachel. The Claytons — and, now, that other girl, Bertha. Yesterday she'd searched for the Claytons in the big blue family book. Deborah was born in 1920. Bertha was born in 1921, and died in 1929. It didn't say what happened, just that she was buried in the Friends' Cemetery in Dallas County, Iowa. Everyone must have been so sad. Bertha had looked like a happy little girl, not just a baby who …

Alyssa shivered. Charlotte's ashes were in Mom and Dad's bedroom. Sometime, they would be buried. In Iowa, Martha Clayton had seemed so sick. Was her baby going to die too? Below Charles's name in the book, there was an entry for Alice Emma Clayton, born in 1931. While everybody else had something written after their names, the space beside the baby was blank. It was too spooky!

Warren Stanley was looking at her. He had such a nice expression on his wrinkled face, and the sunlight was still in his hair. Alyssa tried to smile. He smiled back.

She didn't know where to look next so she focused on the calendar and the red machine with all the spiky things. It looked like it was for plowing fields. But … the April page had been a picture of a tractor. It was May already. The genealogy project was due soon!

Why couldn't she have famous ancestors like Thomas Alva Edison, or Alexander Graham Bell? Or Henry Ford? Then her report would be easy. It would be interesting to write about the Claytons — but what had they contributed to today's way of life? The Underground Railroad idea came back so strongly that it made her look over at Mom and Dad. They'd never find out....

The room grew quieter. Ethan sneezed in a big splat of sound. Somebody laughed in a quiet, friendly way. Alyssa traced her feet in swirls on the rug. Dad glanced at her and his mouth got tight. Alyssa sighed and slumped back in her chair. The wall clock said there was still twenty minutes left before meeting ended. Why did it have to go for a whole hour? *Tick, tick, tick.* She watched the second hand jump ahead and circle its way around the clock face.

Warren Stanley was holding very still. With his eyes closed, he said in his big, gentle voice, "Jesus taught us to love one another. In our silence we wait, listening for guidance about how we can carry God's light in our own small, simple ways. We are challenged to live our faith, so that our lives may speak. If we follow the true leadings of the spirit, our lives will shine with love, honesty, and oneness with all others."

A peaceful sigh went through the room. Suddenly it wasn't so hard to sit. Alyssa looked at Warren Stanley, and thought about what he'd said. When meeting ended and everyone shook hands, a new idea zinged through her. Other people were talking to Warren Stanley, so she waited.

Warren Stanley noticed. "Do you have something to say, Alyssa?" he asked.

Her mouth was dry. "Can there be another peace march?"

He didn't laugh. "I don't decide those things, my friend," he said. "If you'd like, I'll find out if anything's in the works. How does that sound?"

She nodded. When she looked at the other grown-ups, Dad smiled at her.

Rachel's phone rang and rang. "Rachel," Alyssa said to the answering machine. "It's me, and it's Sunday afternoon. Can you go to the library?" Dad and Mom weren't nearby, so probably they wouldn't hear. Why should they keep her from talking to her best friend? All she was phoning about was the school project.

Rachel didn't call back. Ethan was playing a computer game, and turned grouchy when she kept asking to see if Rachel had sent any messages. Nothing came through, and after a while Ethan wouldn't let her check anymore.

Dad was outside, digging in the garden. Last year Mom had done it. Dad's face was wet with sweat when Alyssa went out to talk to him, but he didn't look stressed. She could smell the fresh smell of the dirt. A robin perched on the fence. "Dad?" she said.

He turned around in a hurry. The robin scolded and flew away. Dad laughed a little. "You surprised me," he said.

"Can I go to the library?" Alyssa nudged her toes into the turned-over earth. "I have to do some research for my project."

Dad breathed out sharply. "Always that project," he said. "I'm tempted to tell your teacher how much trouble that project's been causing."

"No!" Miserably, she looked up at him.

"Well?" he said. "You mention it at the strangest times — like four in the morning, when you should be in bed asleep. What would Mrs. Fraser say if I told her you used it as an excuse for your disappearance the other night? We were frantic. So was Lori Lowell."

It was all turning out wrong. "I just want to get it done," she mumbled. "It's due next week." A scared sizzle shot through her. She always turned things in on time. It was never like this — with the deadline almost here, and no idea what she was going to do. It would be wrong to lie about the Underground Railroad — but it was so tempting.

Dad's blue eyes were looking right at her. He didn't seem in a hurry to get back to digging.

Alyssa swallowed hard. "So — can I interview *you*? About what your ancestors contributed our way of life?"

Dad laughed and whacked the shovel into the dirt. "Sure," he said. "If you want to talk about how to run a sewage treatment plant. You know that's what Grandpa Dixon did before he retired, don't you?"

Alyssa felt her mouth twitch. "Yeah. And that's why you're a college teacher instead." If Mom were her usual self, she might actually think about it; it was a brave kind of topic. But right now it was too scary. Already she could imagine Brooklynne snickering, and the awful whispers. "What about Grandma?" she persisted.

Dad shook his head. "She was always busy taking care of the family. It's sad; she never had much time for herself, and even now she doesn't because of your grandpa's bad back. Is that the kind of thing your teacher wants?"

"Not really." Great-Grandpa Dixon had been a truck driver. There was nothing wrong with those kinds of jobs; it was just that they were so obvious. The report would have to be about Mom's side of the family.

A robin sang in one of the trees; it sounded like sunshine coming out in little twists of music. Alyssa stretched. "So can I go to the library?" she asked.

Dad picked up the shovel. "I don't see why not," he said. "I'll take you. How about helping me finish up here, first?"

How come? she almost asked. But Dad's face was sweaty. Dirt was streaked across his forehead and his neck was sweaty. Usually Mom did the gardening. Dad didn't seem grumpy about doing it. And in Iowa ... Deborah and her brothers and sisters did so much work. How could she say no?

Alyssa got the extra garbage can for Dad, and several black garbage bags. Then she sat down and pulled the long white weed roots out of the dirt after Dad dug. Pink earthworms wriggled in the loosened clumps of soil. She touched one and smiled at its cool, slithery feel.

"So," Dad said. "You'd like to go to another peace march?"

"Yeah," she said. "It's something kids can do."

"That's my girl, Lyssa." It sounded like Dad was smiling.

When a big section of the garden was dug, they took Mom's car to the library. Alyssa noticed little crumbs of dirt clinging to Dad's shirt. There were wet circles under his arms. She checked her hands. She'd washed them, but the blue nail polish was scratched and worn. Wedged beneath her fingernails was dark, crusted dirt. She picked at it until only a tiny bit showed.

Dad was quiet as he drove. Alyssa noticed dirt under his fingernails too. When he stopped for the red light at Hartford Street, he turned to her. "Lyssa." He sounded incredibly sad. "Why can't you tell us about Friday night?"

She stiffened. "I told you over and over!"

"Are you worried something might happen?"

Alyssa leaned forward, stretching the seatbelt. "I *told* you. I went to Iowa. It was 1931, and Martha Clayton was going to have a baby pretty soon. She looked really sick. Mom never looked like that."

A car with loud, thumping music caught up with them in the next lane. Dad sighed. "What, exactly, do you plan to do at the library?"

"What do you think? Look for books. And go on the computer, since Ethan's hogging ours. All because of his stupid game."

"Books on what? What will you look for on the computer?"

"Iowa, I guess. I don't exactly want to research the history of sewers. Who wants to give a report on poop?" She knew she shouldn't have said it, but it just came out.

Dad's mouth tightened. "I'll come in with you," he said.

The library was busy. All of the computers were in use, so Alyssa signed up for the next available one. Dad sat down in the section with the newspapers. Alyssa noticed that wherever she went, he seemed to be watching her. Resentment flared through her as she wandered up and down the aisles. Didn't Dad trust her?

There were only two books on Iowa in the children's section. Alyssa took them off the shelf and sat at a table that was behind Dad's back. Chatham was there, a tiny dot near Des Moines on one of the maps. Corn and soybeans ... Hogs, cattle and sheep ... The earliest explorers were French — that wouldn't work for her report. Her ancestors wouldn't have fought the Indians ... She couldn't find anything about the Underground Railroad. President Herbert Hoover came from Iowa ... He was a Quaker! And he'd been president in 1931! Excited, Alyssa wrote down the names of his relatives. Maybe they'd be in the big family book! If they were, her report wouldn't be so hard after all.

"Look at the brown-noser. Even on a Sunday — always sucking up to the teacher."

Alyssa tensed. Not Brooklynne! She checked the clock and went straight to the computers. It was time for her turn — and the library would close before her half hour was finished.

"Excuse me," she said to the teenager who was checking her messages. "I'm signed up for this computer."

The girl didn't even look up. "Just a sec," she said vaguely.

But it wasn't just a second. The girl sat there, typing and swirling strands of her long hair as she read.

"Um ..." Alyssa tucked the books against her side. "Excuse me, but the library's closing soon. My time was supposed to start five minutes ago."

The girl scowled at her. "Chill out, will you? What's a minute or two?"

Alyssa gulped in a frantic breath. What should she do? Get a librarian?

"Hey, Brandi." Brooklynne sidled up to the computer. Her shiny blond hair jiggled on her shoulders as she shoved against the girl. "Scoot over. I need to send something." She looked straight at Alyssa, flashing her braces in a fake smile. Her eyes gleamed like hard, polished stones.

Alyssa's stomach froze. Brooklynne and the teenager looked like they might be sisters. Why had she bothered trying to stand up for herself? What was Brooklynne going to do?

Meanwhile the girl, Brandi, grimaced. "Just a minute!" she snapped.

Suddenly Dad was nearby, watching. So was one of the librarians. *Go away!* Alyssa thought hard at Dad, in his dirty work shirt ... That was the last thing she wanted Brooklynne to see. Maybe the librarian would say something.

Brooklynne reached across her sister and grabbed the mouse. She opened a new message, keying in somebody's address. Then she looked at the toolbar and changed the font.

ALYSSA STINKS. For a long, terrible instant, the words sat there on the screen in huge red letters. Then, with a click of the mouse, they vanished. The message was sent.

Alyssa squeezed her lips together, but that didn't stop tears from spilling down her cheeks.

"You do, you know." Brooklynne looked pointedly at Alyssa's front.

She couldn't help checking her shirt. There, on her stomach, was a smudge of dirt from the garden. She tried to hold her head up proudly. "I don't need that stupid computer," she said. But it came out choked with crying.

The librarian was saying something to Brooklynne. Alyssa turned away.

Dad's arm came around her. "Let's go home, Lyssa," he said quietly.

They headed for the door. Then the alarm beeped because she hadn't checked out the books. Sniffling, Alyssa dug in her purse for her library card. The librarian at the checkout said something to Dad, but Alyssa was too upset to pay attention.

Once they were outside, Dad's arm settled around her again. "Who was that girl?" His voice was grim.

"Brooklynne Bayne." It hurt to talk. "Only the mayor's daughter. And the new TV anchorwoman's." Then her foot hit a concrete parking block. She pitched forward.

Behind her came the sound of mocking laughter.

Dad spun around. By the time Alyssa was on her feet again, he was halfway back to the building. But Brooklynne had vanished.

Chapter Twelve

Rachel didn't come to school the next morning. A quivery feeling kept darting through Alyssa's stomach as she sat at her desk. She didn't dare look across the room, toward Brooklynne and Mackenzie. The message at the library was too awful! Who did Brooklynne send it to? Mackenzie? Or did she send it to a lot of people?

"Class," Mrs. Fraser said, "we have a very important date next week." Mrs. Fraser's hair was cheerful and fluffy … not like Mom's. When she wrote May 13 in neat yellow cursive letters on the chalkboard, everybody groaned. Mrs. Fraser turned around to face them. "I expect every one of you to give your very best effort to this project," she said. "It's the most important thing you will do in sixth grade. In addition to researching, displaying, and talking about information that may not always be easy to find, you have been developing long-range organizational skills."

Alyssa doodled in her notebook as Mrs. Fraser's voice droned on and on. "… Next year … seventh grade … junior high … genealogy project … *very* important part ... grade for social studies ..." Alyssa's pencil stalled on a bird doodle as the smooth swish of chalk told her that Mrs. Fraser was writing on the board. "Geography ... Language arts ... Communication skills ..." There were snappy *tics* as Mrs. Fraser dotted each *i* and crossed the *t*s. "... Citizenship ... report card." Alyssa's face burned. Mrs. Fraser wasn't being fair! The doodled bird grew a gigantic claw that reached into the middle of the page.

"As always," Mrs. Fraser continued, "... top five projects ... Kennedy School Citizen of the Year Award ... something new. I want all of you — *all* of you, Seth ... keep ... research ... find something ... Internet ... print it out. Mr. Bergman ... class assembly based on your reports."

The quivery feeling in Alyssa's stomach turned into a cold, heavy rock. She looked up at the flag hanging in the corner, and at the picture of the president. The classroom lights glinted on the circle of foil stars around him.

"... Quite an honour ... take our principal's invitation seriously ... when our freedom is so much at risk ... proud ... my students ... set a good example for the younger children here at Kennedy School."

The display of war medals sat on the wall like a cluster of Mrs. Frasers, each one staring right at her. Now the words on the bulletin board said AMERICA — HOME OF THE BRAVE. The wall by the door was covered with artwork of soldiers, guns, and flags. Some of the boys had drawn tanks and planes, and bombs exploding. Way off to the side where people wouldn't notice them were two American eagles. One had her name in the lower right corner; the other had Rachel's. Where *was* Rachel?

In Alyssa's notebook, the doodle bird that had started out beautiful was now ugly.

"Tristan," Mrs. Fraser said. "How is your project coming?"

"Um …" The boy fumbled through his papers. "Okay, I guess."

"Good. Matthew?"

Would Mrs. Fraser go down the rows and ask everybody? Alyssa started writing fast, making things up and jotting down whatever came to mind.

"Alyssa." She jumped. "How is your genealogy project coming? Have you decided on a topic yet?"

Alyssa's heart pounded. "Yes," she said. Her voice got stronger. "I'm writing about the Underground Railroad. Some of my ancestors helped with it."

Mrs. Fraser actually smiled at her. "How interesting! We'll look forward to hearing more." Then, just as suddenly, her face froze into a tight mask. "*Which* Underground Railroad?" she asked. "You aren't talking about the Vietnam War, by any chance, are you?"

Alyssa's hands shook so badly that her pencil clattered onto the floor. "No." A huge, trapped feeling surrounded her. Maybe this was what "dread" was like. She took a deep breath. "My ancestors helped slaves escape to Canada. Before the Civil War."

With luck, maybe it would be true.

★

Rachel came to school the next day, but she was quieter than usual. Alyssa felt so keyed up about Brooklynne's bullying and about her report that she didn't think to ask why. Should she tell Rachel about lying about her family history? But she couldn't seem to get Rachel alone to talk about it. Besides, Rachel had to leave school early; the music festival was on, and she was playing her clarinet in several competitions.

In desperation one afternoon, Alyssa spread all of her things out on the dining-room table. She flipped through the big blue book. Herbert Hoover wasn't in it, so she couldn't talk about the things he did when he was president. She found the Claytons' page, with Deborah — who ended up marrying somebody named James Albert Newlin. Then she found pages about George's parents, and about Martha's parents, the Goodens. There wasn't anything about Martha's grandparents, but the book was full of Claytons. There were so many of them that it was impossible to figure everyone out. There were Claytons in Iowa, and Claytons in England. There were Claytons in Australia. Somebody she'd never heard of had been a missionary in Japan. There was a Clayton born in 1702. "Mom?" she called. "Can you help me?"

The only answer she heard was a thumping sound. Mom must be doing something in one of the closets. Alyssa picked up the heavy book and wandered around the house, looking. Mom wasn't in the baby's room. She wasn't in Alyssa's room, either. Alyssa hesitated at the doorway of her parents' bedroom. Clothes were heaped on the bed. Boxes and suitcases were jumbled about. Alyssa's heart skipped a beat. "Mom! What are you doing?"

Mom jumped. She was wearing a t-shirt and baggy jeans — in fact, they were Dad's clothes. Her hair was dirty again. Her face had a frustrated, unhappy look. "Nothing fits."

Alyssa didn't know what to say. She dropped the genealogy book on the bed. It slid off and thudded onto the floor, along with Mom's pretty tank top covered with pink roses and a pair of white shorts.

"What do you want?" Mom's voice made it sound like Alyssa was just one more job she had to take care of.

Alyssa felt like stomping away — but only Mom could help her. "I need you to explain some things," she said. "For my genealogy project."

"What do you need to know?"

"This book!" Alyssa opened it to Deborah's family's page. "There's too many Claytons! It says George Clayton was born near Chatham, Iowa, in 1895. But who were his parents? There's two Edwin Claytons. And who are the ones that came from England?"

"Let's check our entry," Mom said. "This is so complicated." She flipped through the pages. And there they were — Jennifer Sarah Hadley married to Gregory Thomas Dixon, with Ethan Gregory and Alyssa Claire.

Alyssa shivered, remembering the blank spot on Deborah's page beside the baby Alice, who was born in 1931. Really, there should be a place for Charlotte too. Charlotte Jane Dixon.

Mom seemed to be thinking the same thing, for she sat down with the book in her lap and closed her eyes for a moment. "What are you going to write about?" she asked.

"I don't know." She didn't dare tell Mom what she'd told Mrs. Fraser.

Mom turned more pages. "There must be some stories in here. Oh, look — Edwin Clayton and his family moved to Iowa from England in 1873. He walked two hundred miles and back to look at their farm, before they bought it and moved there. That's kind of interesting."

"But what does that have to do with our way of life?" Alyssa asked. "Didn't anybody help with the Underground Railroad? Mrs. Fraser won't let me talk about peace." Again, she thought of how Mrs. Fraser had looked at her in class that day when she'd asked about the Vietnam War.

Mom didn't say anything for a while. "Maybe Dad should phone Mrs. Fraser," she finally said.

"No!" Alyssa grabbed the book and went back to the dining room.

She opened her notebook. *Edwin Clayton,* she wrote. *Walked 200 miles to see the farm. Moved from England in 1853.* Her hand shook a little bit. But if she wrote it enough times, maybe it would start to seem true.

She checked the pictures Mom had found. Was there one of Edwin Clayton? The writing was faded and hard to read, and her eyes were tired.

Sounds of explosions came from the computer downstairs. Ethan shouldn't be playing war games! Alyssa went to the basement to talk to him.

"Can you look some stuff up for me on the Internet?" she asked.

"Why?" Ethan's hand and the mouse kept moving.

Alyssa stomped her foot. "For my report. All you ever do is play games, and I need to use the computer."

Ethan sighed, and then yelled as a red blast obliterated the screen. "Now look what you did! You just made me die."

"I'm telling ..."

"Okay, okay. What do you need?"

"Relatives." Alyssa showed him the Clayton page in the book. "I need things on the Goodens."

Her brother's fingers were fast on the keyboard. "There's *thousands*," he said. "Way too many to look at. What state?"

"Iowa. In Chatham."

Ethan stared at her. "Are you moving there or something? That's all you ever talk about."

"*Please?*"

"Nothing on Goodens. And there's millions of Claytons. I'll check for you later, okay?"

"Ethan...."

His fingers were speeding over the keyboard again. Alyssa saw Ethan's name typed into the search area. "Hey, cool!" he said. "Look how many other people have my name!"

"Check me." Alyssa leaned closer. She held her breath as her own name appeared in the box.

"Huh?" Ethan clicked the first link on the page.

ALYSSA DIXON it said at the top of a web page. The

background was an icky barf colour. "She thinks she is so smart. Everybody knows we all hate her." Her class picture was there, smiling — but somebody had made her teeth look rotten. There was a big mole on her nose, with a hair growing out of it. Her hair … In her class picture, it was shiny and neat. Here, it was messy. There were white dots in it. "Lice," it said, with an arrow pointing to one of the blobs. "Keep away from Alyssa. Bad breath," it said someplace else, with another arrow. "B.O. Alyssa has smelly B.O., stay away." The website had links. "See Alyssa crying. See Alyssa naked. See Alyssa tied up with poop on her face."

"*Huh?*" Ethan said.

Alyssa couldn't say anything. Her throat had seized up so tightly it was hard to breathe. Cold sweat covered every bit of her skin.

"Lyssa…." Ethan's hand touched her shoulder and gave her an awkward pat. "I'll tell Dad, okay?"

A sob wrenched from her. Alyssa stumbled up the basement stairs, and then hesitated. If she went to her room, Mom would probably notice. Did she want Mom? The garage would be safer.

Why couldn't she find her backpack? And the picture, with the magnifying glass?

Chapter Thirteen

Alyssa cried in the garage until her nose was so stuffy she felt like she might choke. Even then it wouldn't stop. Shaking, she leaned against Mom's locked car. Strange noises kept coming out of her. One of the links had said "See Alyssa naked." What had they put there? Had everybody seen it? She doubled over and curled into a tight ball on the cold cement floor. Her teeth chattered. Why couldn't she just … die? She slammed her head against a hard object, which slid sideways — the snow shovel, she realized.

And still she couldn't stop crying. After a while a weird feeling came over her — old, tired … dead. Maybe she should drink something poisonous. Windshield washer fluid? But she couldn't stop shaking. Her teeth pounded like hammers; every jolt moved the hurting muscles in her face. It was easiest not to breathe, but her body always took over and gulped in a huge gasp.

"Lyssa?" Somebody tugged at her.

"Leave me alone!" she wailed.

"Lyssa!" The person didn't leave — and in fact was pulling her up.

She lurched, trying to get free. The person staggered off balance. The thought of falling onto cement kept her from trying again.

"Crap." The person was panting — it was Ethan, and he was saying more things — things Mom and Dad wouldn't want to hear. Now he was hugging her. Alyssa felt her head jiggling against her brother's shoulder. Slowly, the violent shaking stopped.

Ethan backed off. "Hey," he said. "I emailed the server."

She nodded. The awful images kept swarming in her mind. It would be too easy to start crying again.

"Do you want me to get Mom?" he asked awkwardly.

She shook her head. "I just want to ..." Die? Do something awful to Brooklynne? Disappear forever into 1931? Here, she'd have to face Brooklynne. And sit in class every day with Mrs. Fraser being unfair.

The garage windows were cobwebby, but even so, sunlight slanted across the tools hanging from their hooks on the wall and onto Ethan's tousled hair. He fidgeted with the lawnmower handle. "I reported it to the server," he said again. "They'll probably take down the site. Who do you think did it?"

"Brooklynne Bayne. Probably *everybody's* seen it!" No wonder Rachel hardly talked to her at school. Alyssa sagged against the ladder.

"I'll get Mom," Ethan said.

"No. She's too ..." Useless? Too sad already? Mom might freak out. But — what if she didn't do *anything*?

She might not, and that would be worse. Alyssa gulped in a deep breath. "Tell Dad, okay? When he gets home." Strength crept back into her as she spoke. Dad would know what to do — and he *would* do something. He'd seen Brooklynne's message at the library. He was already mad.

"So what're you going to do?" Ethan rapped his knuckles against a tire. "Want me to look up those Clayton people for you?"

This wasn't like Ethan. Usually he'd have gone straight back to play his game, or message the people he talked to online. "No!" The computer was the last place she wanted to be. "Not right now," she added. "Could you get me a chocolate bar or something?"

"What're you going to do? Just wait here? In the garage?" Ethan's direct grey eyes wouldn't stop looking at her.

"No."

"Get your bike," Ethan said. "We'll go to Bristow's."

That wasn't like Ethan, either. "I look awful!"

"Nah. Your eyes are red, but so what? Who do you expect to see at Bristow's?"

"Brooklynne." The incident with the eggs came back full force. Alyssa flipped a wiper blade on Mom's car.

Ethan muttered something. Then he stood straighter. "I know someplace she won't be." He scuffed his foot. As usual, his toes stuck through the holes in his shoes. Parts of the soles had come off completely.

"Where?"

Ethan scuffed harder until his sole folded completely backwards. "Look at this," he said. "I didn't make the cut for the track team because of these stupid shoes. There's a meet right now. I bet I could've placed in the hurdles."

"Oh." She'd forgotten Ethan had things bad, too. But nobody had done a website about him....

"So," Ethan said. "Want to go to the thrift shop? The parents sure aren't noticing what we've got to wear, so I guess it's up to us."

Alyssa thought about her tight clothes. About the stains that hadn't washed out. Maybe she really did look dirty. Did her clothes smell? Did *she*? The website had said ... And the way her scalp got itchy sometimes — *did* she have lice? More tears slid down her cheeks.

"Do you want to? I've still got my allowance. Have you spent yours?"

Alyssa shook her head.

"We can take the bus. Mom won't notice we're gone. Dad teaches tonight...."

Alyssa wiped her face. "It seems wrong, just to go."

Ethan stared at her. "Isn't that what you did?"

"I didn't disappear on purpose! And I was in Iowa."

Ethan shook his head. "Whatever."

The wait at the bus stop went by in a blur. Alyssa kept her face averted so people in cars wouldn't see who she was. Kids from school might be in those cars — and maybe they'd seen the website. The images and words kept streaking through her mind. She almost didn't notice the bus stopping. Later, when it was time to get off, Ethan had to nudge her.

Brooklynne wasn't at the thrift shop, and Alyssa didn't recognize anyone else there. The old clothes had a musty smell. Ethan didn't seem to notice as he tried on shoes. Alyssa wiggled her cramped toes. Her shoes were so tight. She rummaged through the girls' tennis shoes but only found one pair that fit. They were pink, and cost almost as much as she had in her pocket. "Go ahead," Ethan said. "I'll buy those for you."

They wandered down the aisles. "Get yourself some stuff," Ethan said. "It's all pretty cheap, and you definitely need more things to wear."

So even her brother had noticed that her clothes didn't fit. If Ethan noticed, what did everybody at school think? Alyssa found three tops, a pair of jeans, and some shorts. Then she remembered — Deborah must be missing her dress. Could she sew? Probably, but did she have time? The Claytons lived a long way from town. Could they afford more material? Alyssa wandered over to the racks of dresses.

"What do you want a dress for?" Ethan asked.

"Because."

"I haven't got *that* much cash." He slapped his new shoes against the palm of his hand.

None of the girls' dresses looked right for Deborah. Alyssa fingered the cloth. Should she get something that would look strange in 1931? She went on to check the women's dresses, with Ethan trailing far behind. The women's dresses weren't right either. But finally she found one with little blue flowers and buttons down the front. It was an old-lady dress, and it was cheap. Before she could change her mind, she took it off the rack.

When they got home, the pile of newspapers that had been sitting just inside the front door was gone. So was Mom. Alyssa found the note on the messy kitchen counter:

> Gone to drop off some recycling — I need to get out for a bit. I might have coffee with Heather. If you're hungry, you can heat up something from the fridge, or check the freezer.
>
> Love, Mom.

Alyssa stared at her brother. Mom must be getting better!

But Ethan sighed. "Heat up *what* from the fridge? And the freezer's got frozen buns and fish, and a monster ham that's been there for ages. And lima beans. I'm *not* having another peanut butter sandwich for supper."

"Let's order a pizza." It just seemed to blurt itself out. It had been ages since she'd had pizza.

"And pay for it with what?" Ethan said.

"The emergency cash?" Alyssa dropped her bag of new clothes and looked in the canister next to the rice, at the small pile of bills and coins.

Ethan reached past her to scoop it out. "There's enough. They won't mind."

"What kind should we get?" she asked. "Hawaiian?"

Ethan pretended to pout. "*I* want pepperoni, with lots of mushrooms."

The look on Ethan's face made Alyssa laugh. "Okay. We'll get half and half." She gave the bag of clothes a gentle kick. A shirt spilled out, and Marigold came over to investigate. She scooped him up and held his purring body against her cheek.

While Ethan was ordering the pizza, she dug out the rest of her clothes. The pink shoes looked new and even smelled new. She was so lucky — nobody would ever guess they'd come from a thrift shop. Marigold batted at the clean white laces. Alyssa held the shoes at one angle and then another. She stiffened.

"These were Brooklynne's!" she wailed. There it was, written inside each shoe: BROOKLYNNE BAYNE. She couldn't wear them to school!

"Lemme see." Ethan reached for the shoes. "All you need is a good marker. Nobody could tell."

"They could." Alyssa ran to her room and slammed the door. She hardly recognized the face that stared back at her from the mirror. Her hair was messy. Just like on the website.... She yanked her hairbrush through it so hard her scalp hurt.

As usual, dirty clothes were scattered everywhere. A lot of them didn't fit. Alyssa picked up armfuls and stuffed them in the wastebasket. Then she glanced at the picture of herself and Marigold tucked into the corner of the mirror. She looked so happy.... Instant tears spilled down her cheeks. "Why?" she yelled. "I hate *everything!*"

Ethan banged on her door and walked in without waiting for her to answer. "Look," he said. He held the shoes in front of her. Now her name was written inside, with black marker. "Okay?"

"I can't wear anything that was Brooklynne's." Alyssa felt her mouth contorting.

Her brother tossed the shoes on the floor and walked out. His footsteps had a sharp, angry sound.

The house was horribly silent.

"Ethan!" she yelled.

He didn't answer. The TV came on.

"Ethan?" She went to the living room. Her brother was slouched on the couch, and didn't look up when she came in.

"Eeth...." She sat beside him. "Hey ... thanks. For everything." The commercial for cars was so loud she didn't know if he heard.

Ethan scuffed his heel against the rug. "Whatever." He flicked the remote and the volume went down. Then he shoved the coffee table, hard, with his foot. Newspapers, books, and dirty dishes all jiggled. "Know what?" he said. "Sometimes I hate everything too. Everything really sucks, you know?"

The doorbell rang.

"Except pizza," Ethan amended.

Alyssa got the money from the canister. The mouthwatering aroma wafted from the box as she paid the delivery woman.

"Have a good evening," the woman said.

"Thanks," Alyssa said. "You too."

"Pizza!" Ethan yanked up the lid of the box. "Oh, pizza, I love you!"

Marigold agreed. He meowed and looked solemnly at the pizza, then rubbed against Ethan's legs.

"And *you're* not having any," Ethan said. "It's all for me and Lyssa."

"He can have a taste."

Ethan stood there inhaling. "Pizza fumes!" he said. "The best smell in the world." He glanced her way. "Let's eat on the couch."

Alyssa plopped down beside her brother, who was helping himself to two large pieces. The mozzarella cheese stretched in long, dangly strings. "Save some for me!" Instead of waiting, she lurched forward and claimed a piece. There was lots of pineapple buried under the cheese; it sat there like little yellow islands in the middle of a cheese-and-tomato sea. The first bites were awesome. Alyssa sagged back, immersed in the rich flavours and an almost-forgotten feeling of comfort. Then she had to shoo Marigold away because he was licking her greasy fingers, then clawing at her pizza.

Later, she'd look for her backpack and the picture of Deborah and her family. For now, all she wanted to think about was pizza. It was like a celebration — of what, she didn't know, except that it was something she and her brother had done completely on their own.

The hate website seemed a little further away now. Why would Brooklynne go to all that trouble?

Alyssa went to the kitchen and brought back the gallon jug of milk.

"Thanks," Ethan said. He reached, and drank straight from the jug.

"Hey!" Alyssa grabbed the milk. A sudden rebellion swept through her. She held the jug and drank. Milk dribbled down her chin, onto her front. It was cold. But none of that mattered. Her shirt was old, tight, and stained. Later, she'd put on one of the new ones that Ethan had helped buy.

Would Deborah like the dress? She wondered. She'd have to find the picture — *soon*.

Chapter Fourteen

Dad was furious about the website. Alyssa never knew what he actually saw, because soon afterwards the site was gone. Somebody traced it to one of the computers at the library.

Dad looked at Mom. "So, now what do we do?"

Mom was reading in the comfy chair. She sighed. "I don't know. Call the library, I guess." After a long, clinging hug when Mom first found out, Alyssa had the feeling Mom didn't want to think about the website. And that was fine. Alyssa didn't want to think about it either.

At the dining-room table, pretending to work on her genealogy project, she watched Dad fling down the newspaper. "We can't just let it go," he said. "I'm phoning the school."

"No!" Alyssa protested. How could she sit there in a conference with Dad and Mrs. Fraser, and maybe Ethan and the principal too, and talk about the website? Or in class, with Brooklynne right there, if Mr. Bergman talked on the intercom about bullying? What if there was an assembly? What if everybody had to take notes home? It would be awful!

"What about phoning the mayor?" Ethan yelled from the kitchen, where he was fixing a snack. "It's his daughter that did it. Phone the TV station and ask the new anchor lady if she knows what her kid does online. What about the police? The newspaper might be interested."

Alyssa shivered deep in her stomach. At Quaker meeting, people sometimes talked about "speaking truth to power." Peace marches were one way of speaking truth to power. Ethan was talking about something really scary. Her hands were sweaty on her pencil. "No!" she said again. "I don't want the whole world to know! It'll make everything worse."

There was instant silence. Then Dad stood up and went to the kitchen. "What, exactly, do you mean, Ethan?" His voice had an edge to it.

"What do you think?" Ethan said.

Alyssa heard the refrigerator door close. "It could mean several very different things," Dad said.

"And maybe I intend all of them." Ethan sounded defiant.

The website was horrible enough. Now, both Ethan and Dad were trying to help her. But why did they have to argue? She looked over at Mom, who seemed to be reading. *Do something!* she wanted to say. Mom used to be good at calming people down and helping them solve problems. Not anymore.

"What proof do you have, Ethan?" Dad asked. "You've suggested some drastic steps. A private discussion and a public accusation are two very different things. What if you're wrong? Things could get extremely messy for all of us — particularly Alyssa. Now that the website's been taken down, we'd have a hard time proving this even happened. And think about the consequences for the Bayne family. They're prominent people in this city."

"All the more reason to expose what their monster of a kid's been doing to my sister." A plastic bag rustled as Ethan spoke. "Besides, I've got proof."

Alyssa went out to the kitchen. Ethan was pouring himself a huge glass of milk. Dad was slicing cheese. Right now they didn't seem mad at each other.

"I saved everything," Ethan continued. "I printed it out from the actual site. All of it, including the links. I got the web address and the dates. It's in the computer history. Want me to email it to you at the college?"

Alyssa felt sick.

Dad must have felt something too, because he leaned against the counter with his face averted. She looked at his back, long and smooth in a dark blue shirt. When he turned around again, a muscle in his jaw was twitching. "Jennifer!" he called. "What do you think about this?"

Mom's slow footsteps approached the kitchen. She was still wearing Dad's clothes, and her hair was dirty again.

Alyssa held onto a chair back and took a deep breath. "Why isn't anybody asking me? Don't I have any say?"

A knife clattered onto the kitchen counter. Ethan ran his finger along the blade, wiping off peanut butter, which he licked from his finger.

"What do you think we should do, Lyssa?" Dad smiled at her. Alyssa had the feeling he didn't think she'd come up with a solution.

She nudged her foot against some onion skins that had fallen onto the floor. "Call the library," she said. "I had to sign up to use the computer. Probably they have a record of who goes online. Maybe they'll ban Brooklynne from the computers."

Dad's fingers tapped on the counter top. "Actually, I already phoned the library. I did it after Brooklynne sent that message."

"What message?" Mom and Ethan asked.

"I told you." Dad's voice was curt. He was looking at Mom, not Ethan. "They said they'd talk to her if she wants to use the computers again. I'm sure they're worried about what could happen if Wes and Crystal Bayne took it wrong. City council could easily vote to reduce library funding. The library's already had to cut back on staffing and the number of hours they're open."

What did any of that have to do with the website? Alyssa opened the refrigerator. The cool smell of food washed over her. There wasn't much in there. Supper had been skimpy, just the macaroni and cheese she'd made and salad. There was a little bit of macaroni left. She stuck her hand in the casserole dish and pulled out a clump of cold noodles.

Alyssa ate all the leftover macaroni, and started shaking. Again. It had happened several times since that awful day. Like always, the terrible words and pictures flooded her mind. Probably everybody was laughing at her. Did she have bad breath?

Alyssa's teeth chattered. She went to her room and put on her sweatshirt. KENNDEY SCHOOL PATRIOTS stretched across the blue front. Like almost everything else, it was tight. The pink tennis shoes lay on the floor by her closet. She hadn't worn them. They seemed to laugh at her, as if Brooklynne were right there in her bedroom.

A huge feeling surged through Alyssa. She didn't know what to call it. It wouldn't let her hold still, not with those shoes in her room. She gave them a hard kick. They banged against her closet door. There was a cat yowl. Marigold hissed, and ran out of her room.

She kicked the shoes again. It felt good. Except, all that happened was that Brooklynne's old-new shoes bounced off the closet door, and lay there.

Alyssa picked up a black marker from the pile scattered on her bedside table. She wrote the most horrible thing she could think of to call Brooklynne on the clean pink side of one of the shoes. The ugly word made her feel all dirty inside, the same way the website had. Ethan used his own money to buy those shoes, and then wrote her name in them over Brooklynne's.

Her teeth were still chattering. "Mom," she whimpered.

Something made her think of Warren Stanley's kind face and the way the sunlight made his white hair shine in meeting for worship. She crawled in bed and pulled all of the covers over her head. After a while the crying and shivering stopped.

133

The shoes were still in her bedroom, and now one of them had a word that made her just as bad as Brooklynne. Alyssa wiped her eyes and got up. She stuffed the pink shoes in her wastebasket, underneath the clothes that were already there.

But that word was still in her bedroom. Nobody else might look in her wastebasket, but it was there just the same. If she threw the shoes in the garbage, they might fall onto the street when the garbage truck came. Even at the dump, somebody might find a pair of new pink shoes with that awful word — and her name inside.

She retrieved the shoes. They still smelled new, but now they also smelled like marker. Alyssa felt sick at the sight of the ugly black writing. "I'm sorry," she said. She didn't know exactly why she said it, but it helped. Biting her lower lip, she used the black marker, and then a green one, and a blue one, to make a design. It sort of hid the word. Probably nobody could tell anymore. She drew a different design on the other shoe and felt better.

She looked at her collection of ceramic horses on the shelf and at her books. She used to love reading. On the wall there was the picture of Stardancer that she'd cut out of the girls' magazine that came in the mail every month. "Remember your gift," the words of the song went, "now let your life shine." Except it was "light," not "life."

She glanced at the photo of herself holding Marigold. He must feel under attack, awakened by shoes flying through the air. "Here, kitty kitty," she called. She kept her voice soft. "Marigold...."

There was a faint answering "*mrrauu*" from another room. Alyssa tiptoed into the hall. "Marigold? Where's my kitty?"

"*Mrrauu.*"

It came from the baby's room. Alyssa flicked on the light. The room had a stale smell now, as if Mom had polluted the air, sitting there so much without taking showers or changing her clothes. Alyssa opened the window. The usual cardboard box was on the floor, but only a few things were packed. Little sleepers and shirts, dresses, blankets, bonnets, and bibs, sat folded in stacks on the floor. In one place they were rumpled and scattered. Probably Marigold ran over them when he escaped. A colourful crocheted afghan had been dumped in the rocking chair. "Marigold?" she said again.

"*Mrrrt?*" It came from under the crib.

Alyssa got down on her hands and knees. Huddled against the wall amidst dust bunnies, crumpled tissues, and plastic bags, she saw Marigold's furry shape and round, glowing eyes. "Come here," she said, extending her hand. "I'm sorry. I didn't mean to scare you."

Marigold stood up and came to her. One of his hind feet was caught on something; there was a swish of something dragging behind him.

"Marigold, what have you got there?" Then Alyssa's heart pounded. Familiar blue straps … orange tassel on the zipper.… "My backpack!" She yanked it out from under the crib, covered with golden cat hairs and other fluff.

Marigold's foot was still tangled in one of the cords. He gave an eerie cat moan that turned into a growl, then a hiss. He glared at her with irate green eyes. His striped tail twitched.

"I'm sorry." She extended her hand. Marigold sniffed the fingers that had held the macaroni, then rubbed against her. He arched. Purring, he took possession of her lap.

His simple, forgiving warmth almost made Alyssa cry again. But her backpack … Stroking Marigold, she reached inside. There it was, the bubble envelope containing the picture of the Claytons and the magnifying glass.

She didn't need both hands to pet the cat. With her free hand, she reached into the envelope for the old photograph. Then she picked up the magnifying glass….

Marigold rubbed against her cheek. Laughing, Alyssa snuggled against him. The magnifying glass showed her an enlarged Deborah.

It happened so quickly there was no avoiding it — the intense, paralytic tingling. This time a yowling, struggling presence went with her.

Gasping, she landed on cool grass. It was evening. With a hiss, Marigold launched himself off her stomach and disappeared into the dusk. Soon afterwards a dog barked excitedly. It sounded like Flossie.

"Marigold!" Alyssa screamed.

Chapter Fifteen

Faint sunset colours lit wispy clouds overhead. The sky was darker in the east where a bright star twinkled. Just above the grass, little lights darted and blinked. *Fireflies,* something in her head announced.

"Marigold!" Her voice sounded puny. Where would a terrified cat go in all this open space? Alyssa looked around to get her bearings. There was the house, with a few windows lit, the barn, the silo. There was the chicken coop. The windmill. Nearby, the fireflies continued to dance and dart. For a moment she watched them, fascinated.

There was Flossie, barking and jumping beneath a tree with wide, spreading branches. Marigold had to be there. When she hurried to it, the dog recognized her, sniffing and wagging. A plaintive cat moan came from above.

Two figures came running. "Alyssa!" one of them cried. "Thee's back!"

It was Herbert and Eva. They were wearing night clothes, and each of them had a jar. Herbert skidded to a stop and looked at her expectantly.

After wrecking the pink shoes and after all that horribleness about the website ... What was real? Here, or at home? What happened to all her cells and molecules when she went back and forth? Now Marigold was here too. She hadn't even brought Deborah's dress.

Flossie resumed her barking.

"My cat's up there," Alyssa said. "How can we get him?"

"Thy cat came?" Herbert set his jar down and scrambled up the tree.

Why hadn't she thought of that? Alyssa's stomach smarted where Marigold had scratched her. Beside her, Eva was twisting the lid of her jar. "What's in there?" she asked.

"We're catching lightning bugs." Eva held it out.

Intrigued, Alyssa stared at the beetle trapped behind the glass. Every now and then its abdomen flashed with a cool, yellow-green light. "We don't have those at home," she said.

"Here, puss, puss," Herbert said overhead. There was a hiss, followed by the sound of Marigold retreating even higher. "Ow!" Herbert slid back down and licked a scratch on his hand. "He'll come when he's ready."

"But ..." Marigold wasn't an outside cat; he wasn't used to other animals. She vaguely remembered seeing a scrawny striped cat hanging around the barn. That cat wouldn't want Marigold on his turf.

"I'll get Debbie," Eva offered. When she ran toward the house, Alyssa noticed that she held her nightgown away from her legs.

"We're sleeping outside," Herbert said. "Daddy and Wilfred and Debbie are setting up a bed for Mama on the porch."

The air felt soft and humid. Her school sweatshirt definitely wasn't the right thing to have on. Alyssa peeled it away from her t-shirt underneath. Why couldn't she have come in the morning? Now, like last time, she'd have to go to bed. Then somebody would find the picture, and she'd be yanked back to her messed-up life.

As Herbert ran around chasing fireflies, a hot feeling grew in her chest. She could stay here. She could be another girl in the Claytons' family and help out. There'd be extra work when the baby came.

Her throat tightened as she remembered how things were when Charlotte didn't come home. All the phone calls, the people dropping by to say how sorry they were. The meals that didn't get cooked, the way the fridge and the shelves grew empty and stayed that way except when Grandma Hadley or Auntie Deb was there. The trash that didn't get carried out, the dirty dishes and dirty clothes. All the new baby presents that sat there like a fake celebration.

Alyssa thought of the blank space in the book beside Alice Emma Clayton's name and shivered. Was there a reason why she'd ended up here, in 1931? She remembered what Warren Stanley had talked about in meeting for worship — something about everybody carrying God's light in their own little ways. Could she help make a difference?

At the house, a door banged. "Alyssa!" A moment later, Deborah stood beside her.

Alyssa felt a smile burst across her face. "Hey!" she said.

"It's good to see thee!" Deborah clasped her hand. "I'm so glad to be out of that hot house. Poor Mama isn't well, but sometimes I wish that baby would just hurry up and come so I don't have to work all the time." Then she drew back, looking ashamed. "I shouldn't have said that. It makes me seem ungrateful. Really, I'm not."

"Her name's going to be Alice Emma," Alyssa said impulsively.

Deborah gasped. "How does thee know? But of course — thee's from the future." She brushed sweaty brown hair out of her face. Her feet were bare, and her dress was faded.

"It's in a family book." Alyssa didn't dare tell about the blank space beside the baby's name — or about Charlotte.

It was getting darker. The fireflies darted like bright little exclamation marks above the grass.

Deborah touched her arm. "If it's in a family book, how does thee fit? How are we related?"

"You're not my grandmother. Her name is Anne Hadley." Should she have said that? What if something changed? "I think you're my great-grandmother," she added.

Deborah burst out laughing. "Thy great-grandmother? I'm eleven years old, and thee says I might be thy great-grandmother! This is so ... peculiar!" She looked over her shoulder at the house. "I really should go back, but Daddy and Wilfred can move that bed without me. If only it weren't getting dark. We could go down to the brook to talk."

The air was sweet with smells of grass and other growing things. "How's the crop?" Alyssa asked. "After the hail, I mean. Is it going to be okay?"

"There was some damage, but not …"

"Debbie!" a voice shrieked. "Susannah wants thee to sing."

Deborah sighed. "Frances really thinks that doll is alive. But I suppose I did too, when I was small. I hope this new baby is quiet!"

Alyssa couldn't help smiling. "Want me to sing? I could do more 'la-la somethings.'"

Deborah shouted with laughter and then clapped her hands over her mouth. "Wouldn't she be cross then! Oh, Alyssa, I've figured out words for thy song! Thee must hear them. Come!"

She turned and ran toward the house; Alyssa had no choice but to follow. Running felt so good. Without even realizing it, this was something else she'd missed ever since their lives got turned upside-down.

Frances stood on a blanket spread on the grass. In her pale nightgown, she looked ghostly in the dim light. The big doll lay at her feet. "Sing, Debbie!" she screeched. "Susannah can't sleep."

Deborah settled the doll on a pillow. "Thee's making so much noise, Frances. Is it any wonder Susannah can't sleep?"

Frances shook her head stubbornly. "Susannah doesn't mind me. She needs thee. Or Mama."

Deborah repressed a sigh. "Thee knows Mama mustn't be disturbed. The doctor says ..." Frances plopped into Deborah's lap, and whatever she'd meant to say became an "*umph*."

"Frances, couldn't thee sit down more gently? Thee knows I'm not a chair."

The little girl giggled. "Thee is so a chair. Debbie, the rocking chair." She looked up at Alyssa, and bounced in Deborah's lap.

"Frances! Hold still! If thee doesn't, I won't sing."

Alyssa sat on the blanket. There was another one spread out nearby with a pile of folded sheets and quilts and several more pillows. Flossie padded over to settle beside them. The dog scratched its ear for moment, then lay there contentedly. Was Marigold still up in that tree?

Eva approached. "Charles is on the davenport," she said. "Should he just stay there?"

Deborah sighed. "He'll be sweltering. Thee should bring him out here."

Eva's lower lip trembled. "He might fuss."

Deborah was beginning to look flustered. "Then get Herbert to help thee. This little missy —" she clamped her arms around a giggling Frances "— is far more of a handful than thy little brother."

"I'll go." Alyssa stood up. "I can carry him. Maybe he won't wake up."

The house was stifling. Heat wrapped around Alyssa like a smothering blanket. In the warm kerosene light, she noticed that the windows were open. No wonder the family had decided to sleep outside. Loud thumps came from another room.

Eva tugged at her hand. "He's in here," she said.

Alyssa followed her into the living room. Lamp light glanced off photos of people in old-fashioned clothes. Charles lay on the couch, his face flushed and glistening with sweat. Alyssa felt a tug in her heart as she picked up the hot little boy.

"Mama?" he asked sleepily. His arm came around Alyssa's neck.

"No," said Eva. "It's Alyssa. That strange cousin who visited earlier."

"We're going outside." Alyssa said quietly. "It's too hot to sleep in here." With Eva holding doors open, she managed to carry him without much jostling. As she set Charles on the blanket near Deborah and Frances, he relaxed back into sleep.

Deborah touched her arm. "Thanks for thy help, Alyssa. Frances," she continued sternly, "thee sees thy little brother is sleeping. Thee must be quiet now. If thee can stay quiet, we'll sing to Susannah."

Mom would enjoy Deborah's tactics. Then, suddenly, Alyssa remembered the other picture — the one with Bertha. Sadness settled through her as she looked at Deborah, still sitting patiently with Frances in her lap. Deborah must miss her sister terribly.

The sky grew noticeably darker. Sitting there with the Clayton children, Alyssa realized she felt safe — *completely* safe — for the first time in quite a while. Flossie's relaxed breathing had such a peaceful sound that she was tempted to lie down on the blanket herself.

"Mama's outside," Eva whispered, and headed toward the porch. Herbert, still chasing fireflies, nearly collided with her.

"My poor Eva," Deborah said thoughtfully. "She worries so...."

"I'm being quiet," Frances said in a sweet little voice.

"Thee's being very good," Deborah said. "We'll sing when Eva gets back."

"What's she worried about?" Alyssa brushed a crawly thing off her arm.

Deborah sighed. "We had another sister."

"Bertha," Alyssa said.

"Thee knows?"

"She's in another picture. And the family book."

"She caught the polio two years ago. Poor Bertha ..." Deborah's voice wavered. "Eva had it too and hasn't been the same since. I believe she wonders why she recovered when Bertha didn't. I thought of Bertha when I put words to thy tune."

"Bertha died," Frances said solemnly. "I don't 'member."

It seemed so unfair! Especially now that everybody had polio shots. How would it feel to have a sister you loved get so sick that she was paralyzed and died? "That's so sad," Alyssa mumbled.

Deborah drew in a breath. "We don't understand why things happen. All we can do is to keep on trying to be loving and to do what's right." It sounded like something that might be said in meeting for worship.

Eva returned, and Frances said, "We can sing!"

More stars shone. An owl hooted. A faint clucking came from the chicken coop and then was quiet.

Still holding Frances, Deborah started singing. Alyssa stretched out on the blanket and rested her head on her arms. The songs were the same ones Grandma Hadley used to sing to her at bedtime when she was little! "The Ash Grove," then "Tell Me Why," and "Swing Low, Sweet Chariot." Why had they stopped singing at home?

"Susannah's asleep now," Frances said sleepily. Her head drooped against Deborah's shoulder.

"Then we'll just do one more," Deborah whispered. "Alyssa needs to hear the new words for her song."

"No more 'la-la somethings.'" Frances yawned.

Eva had been very quiet. "Let's sing to Mama," she whispered.

There was a moment of stillness. Although it was quite dark by now, Alyssa knew Deborah was looking at her. "I hope thee doesn't mind what I've done to thy song," she said.

"That song was from a movie. I don't know all the words, anyhow."

They walked softly to the porch, where Martha's shadowy form greeted them. Together, Deborah and Eva began to sing:

> If thee feels sad and all alone
> If thy heart feels made of stone
> Even as the tears begin
> Find courage in the light within

Alyssa's skin prickled. The tune had changed from the *Stardancer* song to something else. *She knew this song!* Mom used to sing it to her when she was little. Especially if she was upset. Sometimes Grandma Hadley had sung it too, when they were all together. Alyssa tried to sing now, but her voice choked. When had Mom quit singing it? Why? Her family needed this song. *She* needed it.

> If some cast stones and break thy heart
> If others shirk, just do thy part
> Even as the tears begin
> Find courage in the light within.

A verse started that she didn't know. Alyssa wiped her eyes.

> When darkness comes from all around
> When loved ones leave without a sound
> Seek in silence for the Divine
> And love and light shall thee entwine.

The ending was familiar. Alyssa cleared her throat and sang with the others:

> Remember His gift, and let thy life shine;
> Remember His gift, and let thy life shine.

They sat there quietly. Frances was breathing with faint, little whistles. Out in a field somewhere there was a low murmur from an animal, and then a short cat argument in the barn. It didn't sound like Marigold.

A hand settled on Alyssa's shoulder. "Welcome, Alyssa," Martha said. "It's nice to hear thee sing. Did Debbie teach thee her new song?"

"I learned it from my mom," she said. "And from my grandma, too."

The night itself seemed to shiver.

"Oh, my," Martha said at last. "Did thee hear that, Debbie?"

"I don't know what to say," Deborah whispered.

"What a lovely thing to find out," Martha said. "Goodnight, my sweethearts." She opened her arms to Eva and then Deborah, for a goodnight hug and kiss. "And thee, Alyssa?" she asked. In the dim light, Alyssa could see that Martha Clayton was smiling.

Alyssa burrowed into her great-great-grandmother's arms.

Chapter Sixteen

"Let's go on the other blanket," Deborah whispered after the others had settled. "There is so much I want to ask thee about!"

Alyssa still felt suspended in time. For the *Stardancer* song to come here, where the words and tune changed into a song she'd known all her life.... And *she'd* brought it! She stood up carefully, avoiding the sleeping Charles, Frances, and Eva. Far away, a dog barked. Flossie answered.

Deborah fluffed two pillows. "I so enjoy sleeping outside," she continued. "Just seeing all of those stars, so far away, seems like a miracle."

Alyssa wasn't ready to talk, not yet. She gazed up at the night sky, thinking about Bertha, who'd looked so much like her own kindergarten picture. *Was* she Bertha, somehow, but ended up with Mom and Dad instead? But that couldn't be. Bertha had died of polio. Besides, there were all those baby pictures, and pictures of her with Ethan. Alyssa traced the smooth shape of her fingernails. Her fingers were long and slender like Dad's, not short like Mom's. Her eyes were blue like

Dad's, not grey like Mom's. There was no way she could be Bertha Clayton.

But she could wish she were. Maybe the picture would go under the crib and get lost with all the dust bunnies and plastic bags and tissues. Dad and Ethan never went into the baby's room, so why would they bother looking under the crib? An excited buzz raced through her.

Light streaked across the sky and then was gone. "A shooting star!" Alyssa whispered. "I haven't seen one since I was little."

"Quick," Deborah said. "Make a wish!"

Please, let everything be all right. Alyssa held her breath, wishing. An owl called from a tree near the barn. The windmill creaked faintly.

"Isn't that amazing," Deborah said. "To think we just saw a piece of burning rock falling through the atmosphere!" She hesitated. "That's what our teacher said at Friends school. Does it sound right?"

"Rock, or metal — probably iron and nickel." It felt so good to be confident about something for a change! "Lots of the meteors we see are about the size of a grain of sand."

"Really?" Deborah gasped. "And yet they make such light!"

"Yeah." Alyssa pulled a sheet over herself and lay back. As the sky darkened, the stars shone with a brilliance she never saw at home. There was the Big Dipper and the Little Dipper. A white gauzy glow must be the Milky Way. The summer night hovered around her, making her feel slow and wonderfully lazy. Then a familiar furry body stepped on her shoulder. "Marigold!"

Purring, Marigold settled on her chest. Alyssa stroked him, feeling his soft, rounded head, his delicate ears, his whiskers tickling her face. Maybe everything really was going to be all right.

"Tell me about thy family and about thy life," Deborah said. "I so want to know!"

So Alyssa told her.

Alyssa woke up with a hard surface beneath her and a stiff neck. The eastern sky glowed pink. Birds chirped and mourning doves called. She could hear cows mooing. A rooster crowed.

A rumpled sheet and abandoned pillow lay on the blanket beside her. Did Deborah have a lot of morning chores?

Alyssa made her way to the outhouse and met Deborah on the way back. They'd fallen asleep talking. Had she told Deborah too much? About Charlotte, and how Mom was so depressed. About the assignment and Mrs. Fraser. And about Brooklynne....

Deborah's grey eyes were clear and direct. "How's thee today?" She was carrying two empty buckets.

"Fine," she murmured. "Thanks for listening, last night." It seemed as if a heavy weight had disappeared. Wilfred went past, heading for the barn. She gestured at the house, the barn, and the chicken coop. "Can I help?"

Deborah smiled. "It's First Day. We don't do a lot before meeting. Eva will see to breakfast. Herbert and Flossie have gone for the cows. Wilfred will be feeding them now. Thee could sit with me while I milk Daisy and Bess — has thee ever milked? I could show thee how."

"I could try." Would Marigold come in the barn? He must be starving. "Have you seen Marigold?"

Deborah shook her head. "There was quite a squabble in the barn before thee woke. This would be a real change for thy friend."

"No kidding." Walking beside Deborah, Alyssa glanced at the faded dress she was wearing. "I'm sorry I couldn't bring your dress. I found another one for you too. I'll bring it next time."

Deborah's eyes lit up. "Another dress? What's it like?"

"Um …" She couldn't call it an "old lady" dress. "There's flowers …"

Deborah studied Alyssa's jeans. "Thee can't wear those to meeting. Maybe thee can borrow something of Mama's."

The barn was a dark, cavernous space steeped with the warm smells of hay and animals. If it weren't for a lantern hanging from a hook on a beam, she'd have trouble seeing at all. She heard George's and Wilfred's voices, and then Herbert's as hay cascaded from the loft.

In a stall, two cows were held in place by a frame. As they quietly chewed their food, Deborah pulled out two wooden stools and showed Alyssa how to wash the udders. Large feet shifted and tails swished. Alyssa drew back. "Don't worry," Deborah said. "Daisy wouldn't hurt thee. Try to feel stillness inside."

Alyssa jumped as a skinny calico cat brushed against her ankle.

"Good morning, mother cat. Thee'll get something soon enough. I need to show my —" Deborah burst into giggles "— great-granddaughter about milking."

Alyssa laughed, watching as Deborah's hands sent streams of milk into the pail. "Now thee try it," Deborah said. "Thee squeezes at the top, and then down."

Gingerly she took a teat in each hand. It was hard to see, with the cow's black-and-white side in front of her. She squeezed but nothing happened. "What if I hurt the cow?"

"Thee won't. Try again."

At Alyssa's second attempt, the cow made a low sound and stepped sideways. "Steady," Deborah said, patting the huge shoulder. "Keep trying," she encouraged. "I still envy Daddy, the way he gets milk to flow."

Alyssa thought of the gallon jugs of milk at home. Who'd have thought it could take so much work to get milk out of a cow? A third try brought a dribble. Then something landed in her lap. Claws penetrated her jeans. "Ow!" she yelped. One of Marigold's ears was bleeding. He dug in harder, and hissed at the cow. Something slapped her cheek and the side of her head — moist and smelly, with the consistency of a tangled mop. "Ewww," she said, wiping her face as the cow's tail retreated.

"I'll finish," Deborah said. "Daisy doesn't know thy cat."

Alyssa stood up, tucking Marigold against her. She stroked him, avoiding his injured ear, but Marigold wouldn't purr. When the cow in the next stall let out a loud bellow, he jumped down and raced out of sight.

The scrawny calico cat reappeared. Alyssa laughed when Deborah aimed a squirt of milk at its face. "They like it," Deborah explained as the cat licked it off. "I thought perhaps thy Marigold might notice and be lured back."

But that didn't happen.

After a breakfast of cornflakes and milk with bread and jam, Alyssa went upstairs to the girls' bedroom to try on one of Martha's dresses. The dress gave her a bizarre feeling of being enclosed in a tent — but Martha's shoes fit.

Deborah and Eva seemed doubtful. "I'm not sure how we'll explain thee," Deborah said. "Maybe I can fix thy hair so thee won't draw quite as much attention."

"My hair?" Then, looking at Deborah's hair clips and Eva's bangs, with the rest cut about chin length, she knew. "Should we put it up?"

Frances ran into the room. "Susannah is nowhere!"

"Hush, Frances," Deborah said. "We're getting Alyssa ready for meeting."

Frances tugged at Martha's dress. "This is Mama's! Thee can't wear Mama's dress!"

Eva pulled her away. "Mama says it's fine. Let's watch Debbie fix Alyssa's hair."

Frances's face brightened instantly. "Fix my hair!"

Did that little girl always have to be the centre of attention? Frances's piercing voice was enough to give anybody a headache! How could Martha stand it?

153

The upstairs bedroom was sweltering; flies buzzed haphazardly. Sweat trickled on Alyssa's scalp. She lifted her hair. "Do you have scissors?" she said. "I'll cut my hair. It's too hot like this."

Deborah and Eva stared at her. "Thee'd cut it?" Deborah said. "How will thee get it straight?"

"Could thee do it for me?" She said "thee" deliberately so that if people talked to her at meeting, she might sound like she belonged.

"Certainly." Deborah's eyes sparkled.

At the first raspy sound of scissors chewing through her hair, Alyssa felt a flash of panic. But it was too late. Brown hair lay scattered on a spread-out newspaper — the *Des Moines Register*, she read sideways. Right away her neck felt cooler, and her head lighter.

At last Deborah stepped back to survey her work. "Oh my," she gasped.

Eva sniffled and ran from the room. "What's wrong?" Alyssa asked, looking in the mirror.

It was as if someone else were looking back at her, through her eyes. Even before Deborah said it, she knew. "Thee looks ever so much like Bertha! I'd better go see to Eva."

Alyssa tilted her head one way, then the other. It was eerie, seeing such a different version of herself. Would people even recognize her at school? A quiet *snicking* sound and a flash of light caught her attention.

Frances was sitting by the window. The scissors blades caught the sunlight again as the little girl held a lock of hair away from her face, and snipped. Brown hair was already scattered on the floor around her.

"Frances!" she said. "You —" But Frances wasn't listening. "Frances, *thee* don't do that! What will your mama say?"

Frances looked up at her. From this position, Alyssa realized how small she was. Hacked bangs hung jaggedly on her forehead, and chopped-off hair stuck up above her left ear. "Thee said thee was going to cut *thy* hair."

What would Deborah do? What would Martha do? Alyssa took a deep breath and led Frances to the mirror. "See what thee did? Do thee like it?" As she spoke, she realized she'd said it wrong.

Frances's little jaw tightened. "Yes," she said. "It's pretty."

Downstairs, a door opened. George spoke to someone: "So good of thee to come. I don't want Martha to be alone."

"Edith Smith is here. It's time to go." Herbert charged up the stairs and burst out laughing. "Frances! What has thee done now?" As he looked at Alyssa, he took a sudden step backwards. "Oh, it's thee, Alyssa." He paused for breath. "Thee looks like my sister Bertha."

"I'm sorry," Alyssa mumbled. That was how it went for others too — first the reaction to Frances's hair, and then a stunned exclamation.

She climbed into the surrey, a carriage with a roof and two seats. It was a tight fit between Herbert and Deborah, who was holding Charles. Wilfred and Eva sat in front; an unusually quiet Frances sat in her father's lap. When Alyssa looked at the old-fashioned car parked near the driveway, Deborah noticed. "Gasoline is expensive," she said. "Daddy only uses the car to go to town." The horses pulled, and the surrey creaked forward. Wilfred was driving.

As they turned from the rutted farm lane onto a wider road, excitement soared through Alyssa. This was the first time she'd been off the farm. What would everything be like?

Fields reached in all directions, split by the dusty road. Trees grew in the lowest areas and farm buildings appeared at intervals. Some of the crops were young corn, while others looked like grain. Cattle and horses grazed. By the roadside, fragrant wild roses bloomed among masses of other white, purple, and yellow wildflowers. Meadowlarks sang. The grinding wheels, the horses' trotting hooves, and the squeaking sounds of the surrey made a relaxing accompaniment. Although the day was hot, the breeze felt fresh on Alyssa's face. When she looked backwards, everything was masked by a cloud of dust.

A dusty smudge on the road ahead became a car. Wilfred slowed the horses, steering them to the side. As the shiny, old-fashioned vehicle *putted* past, Alyssa caught a glimpse of its inhabitants in their Sunday best. A hand lifted in a wave, and then they were gone.

"That's the Russell family on their way to church in Chatham," Deborah said. Charles, in her lap, was swinging his feet. "Does thee understand about meeting? About our silent worship?"

Alyssa wriggled in her cramped position. "My family goes to meeting," she said. At least something was the same! That and the song.

After encountering one more car and two teams of horses taking families to church, Wilfred steered toward a treed area where an assortment of people and vehicles had gathered. The meetinghouse was a white clapboard building situated near a house and another small building that Deborah said was the Friends school. Except for these and the grove of large trees, the farm fields continued uninterrupted. MIDDLE RACCOON RIVER FRIENDS MEETING said the painted sign on the meetinghouse, though there wasn't a river in sight.

Wilfred hitched the horses and Herbert jumped out, racing to a wooden swing set in the grassy area behind the schoolhouse. Deborah laughed. "It's so hard for him to be still."

Martha's loose dress snagged as Alyssa stepped down from the surrey. George steadied her as she and Deborah both worked to free the flowered material. Alyssa looked quickly away from his face, for he, too, seemed uncomfortable with her new appearance.

When she followed him toward the meetinghouse door, Deborah pulled her back. "We sit on the women's side," she said.

"But —" Alyssa indicated Frances, holding her father's hand. The little girl's haphazardly cut hair hadn't improved with the ride to meeting.

Deborah repressed a smile but her grey eyes laughed. "Frances sits with Daddy on the men's side. Surely thee knows why."

Alyssa felt the grin on her face. "Yeah, I think so."

"Frances is a handful." Eva had been so quiet that Alyssa had forgotten she was there. She was holding something made of cloth.

A mother and two girls looked curiously at Alyssa. "How is thy mother, Deborah?" the woman asked.

"She's about the same. I thank thee for asking." Deborah edged away.

"I'll fetch Herbert." Alyssa ran to the swings just as the woman asked about "thy friend." By the time they got back, Herbert pausing often to swat at a bumblebee that was following him, most of the people had gone inside.

Deborah's cheeks were pinker than normal. "I *so* wish I hadn't cut thy hair!" she said. "If I'd known the fuss thy looks would cause ..."

Alyssa touched her arm. "But how could ... *thee* have known? Thee thought thee should, so I'd fit in better."

"Thee's 'theeing' us!" Herbert said exultantly.

"Shhh," Deborah said. "We're late."

"Wait." Eva blocked Alyssa's way. "I told Margaret Knight that thy name is Alice Dixon, and that thee's a cousin visiting from North Dakota."

Alyssa nodded. "Okay. I'll remember."

"I felt so flustered, I couldn't think what to say." Deborah put her arm around Eva's shoulder. "I'm glad my clever sister has her wits about her."

Eva looked up at Deborah with a luminous smile that brought sudden tears to Alyssa's eyes. She'd probably never have a sister. Not now.

Chapter Seventeen

Meeting had already started. Alyssa tried not to stare as she followed the two Clayton girls into the quiet room. The wooden benches made it look like a church, except that in front one bench faced the others. Deborah and Eva silently made their way to an empty spot near the back. Eva, sitting beside Alyssa, unfolded a homemade book with pictures pasted in. Words were hand-printed on every cloth page. Alyssa watched, intrigued, as Eva read. The book contained Bible stories, written in simple language.

The women and girls in front of Alyssa wore light-coloured dresses. A few elderly women sat on the front bench, facing everyone else. A wooden divider ran down the middle of the room. The benches on the other side were filled with men and boys, most of them dressed in white shirts, some with their long sleeves rolled up. Alyssa saw George with Charles on his lap, a wiggly Frances beside them, and Wilfred sitting tall between Frances and Herbert. One man on the front bench had a bushy beard. Alyssa suddenly remembered Warren Stanley in meeting, with the sun shining on his hair. His face had looked so gentle, so *loving*. While these people looked kind and peaceful, they also looked ... foreign.

Homesickness crept through her. She was still in Iowa in 1931. What if nobody found the picture? Mom and Dad must be terribly worried. *Ethan!* she thought hard. *Find the picture!* Outside the open window, green cornfields stretched to a rolling horizon.

She thought of Rachel's cheerful face. Was Rachel mad at her? There'd been no phone calls since the one Dad intercepted, and no text messages. Had Rachel seen the website?

On the men's side of the meetinghouse, one of the old men stood up and said something about faith. Alyssa tried to listen, but he went on and on. A fly kept landing on her arm. After more silence, a woman spoke about being prepared to "meet that of God" in everyone, especially during disagreements.

A woman nearby shifted in her seat. Alyssa noticed curious eyes flicking her way. She ducked her head, but her hair wasn't long anymore and couldn't mask her face. If she looked so much like Bertha, maybe it was best to go sit in the surrey. It didn't seem fair for the Claytons to have to explain, and what if George or one of the boys said something different from what Eva told that woman? With the plan formed, Alyssa whispered to Deborah. Before she could finish, Deborah held her finger to her lips and shook her head. Confused, Alyssa stood up and tiptoed outside.

The surrey was in a shady area near other horse-drawn vehicles. The horses were so big ... Changing her mind, Alyssa veered to the grove of trees. She noticed hollyhocks and orange lilies blooming cheerfully all around the foundation of the meetinghouse.

> If thee feels sad and all alone
> If thy heart feels made of stone
> Even as the tears begin
> Find courage in the light within.

Deborah's words to the *Stardancer* song rushed into her mind. How was it that her Great-Grandmother Newlin, as a girl, could make up words that fit so perfectly for how she felt? When she got home — *if* she got home — she'd sing it to Mom. Maybe it would help.

She thought of Marigold, up in a tree, and the way Herbert had gone after him. The trees here looked so inviting. Hitching up the skirt of Martha's dress, Alyssa hoisted herself onto a low branch and sat there, swinging her legs. Really, she was the luckiest person in the world — to be able to slip out of her own life and meet her great-grandma as a girl! Ethan must be jealous. Rachel would love to come. Maybe even Mom? An idea riveted her.

Eventually, people came out of the meetinghouse. Some of them were her ancestors. Maybe the Claytons weren't doing things that got in the news, but that didn't mean they weren't important. If Mrs. Fraser wanted the class to talk about big contributions, or how their ancestors helped protect freedom, she'd just say that most people didn't get to be famous. And, maybe, that there were different ways of protecting freedom.

Frances skipped to the surrey. Herbert followed, looking uncomfortable in his Sunday clothes. "Thee's not to tease!" Frances shrilled. "Debbie told thee so." Then she backed up. "Lyssa's not here! Susannah is nowhere, and now Lyssa's nowhere too."

Alyssa slid down. "I'm over here." She beckoned.

Herbert got there first. He gave her an assessing look. "Why'd thee leave meeting? Daddy's cross."

Alyssa looked away from his direct brown eyes. "I thought it'd be hard to have to explain. Wouldn't it be best if people didn't see me?"

"But thee left meeting!" There was a trace of envy in his voice.

"I always sit through meeting at home." Alyssa brushed a tiny piece of bark off Martha's dress.

Frances tugged at the skirt. "Daddy's coming," she said.

Was she in trouble? George strode toward them, and Deborah followed with a stricken expression on her face.

Sunlight glinted off the wire rims of George's glasses. He didn't exactly seem angry, but his face looked tense. "Alyssa," he said, "I'd like to speak with thee in the meetinghouse."

Alyssa made herself stand straight. "I'm sorry. I didn't know ..."

"We'll speak inside," he said gently. "The children will be glad for a chance to run around."

Quietly, Alyssa walked beside her great-great-grand-father. Her great-great-grandmother's dress swished around her legs. When other people looked curiously at them, some asking questions, George explained that she was a visitor from North Dakota.

The meetinghouse still held the worshipful silence. George led Alyssa to a bench on the men's side. "My wife and I sat in this meetinghouse as children," he said. "It must seem very strange to thee, with thy different ways, and coming from wherever thee lives."

"Yeah" would sound disrespectful. "It's different," she said. "I like it, actually. We have meeting in an office building."

"Oh?" George seemed surprised.

For a few minutes they sat quietly. Alyssa's heart pounded and sweat trickled down her back. What she'd done seemed like the obvious solution. But, as George had said, she had "different ways."

"I'm sorry," she said, breaking the silence. "I didn't know it was wrong to leave meeting."

"I know thee means well," George said kindly. "Thee must realize, though, that thee sets an example for the younger children. Thee is new and ... interesting."

"I didn't think about that," she mumbled. "I just thought how hard it would be for you — *thee* — to have to explain." Her resemblance to Bertha clearly was upsetting. Would Frances have cut her hair, on her own? "I didn't know Frances would cut her hair," she added. "I guess that's my fault." She waited for George to scold, as he didn't seem the yelling type.

There was another prolonged silence. Alyssa looked at the benches with their dark-coloured wood and homemade cushions. In front, a vase of lilies and daisies sat on a table. She could see sweat glistening on George's forearms. At breakfast the Claytons' house had felt stifling, even with the windows open. How did Martha feel, confined to bed? She must be roasting! Despite the heat, Alyssa shivered. Would the baby — Alice Emma — be all right?

"I understand thee has had some hard times," George said.

"My baby sister died when she was being born." Her throat knotted.

George sighed.

"I hope everything's okay for Martha and the baby," Alyssa said in a rush. "It must've been so hard, when Bertha ..."

He rubbed his forehead. "We can't ever know why such things happen. The best we can do is have faith, so that we can try to keep love in our hearts and act responsibly."

This was the strangest scolding she'd ever had! George Clayton seemed to expect her to think things through for herself and come to the right conclusions.

Act responsibly? What was it like for an extra kid to show up when things were already hectic? And she'd thought maybe she could help. What if her coming made things *worse?* She wished she could dissolve into a little pile of dust on the meetinghouse bench. *Ethan!* she thought. *Get the picture!*

What if it was lost? Or if it didn't work anymore?

Alyssa felt she ought to say something, but words wouldn't come. She longed to be outside. Running across the grass would get rid of the nervous energy — or maybe twirling herself dizzy on the swing Herbert had used before meeting. Instead, she was in this quiet room.

"I never thought about the consequences of coming here," she said slowly. "I never thought how it might make everything harder for you."

Surprisingly, her great-great-grandfather smiled. It was a slow, embracing smile, and warmed the scared places inside. "Thee's quite a special girl," he said. "When thee first arrived, I thought thee was selfish. I'm so glad I was mistaken."

"Thanks." Alyssa swallowed hard. "I don't want to mess things up for your family. Probably I shouldn't come back here again."

"That would be wise, I think." Her great-great-grandfather clasped her hand. "We don't want there to be consequences for thy family, either."

Hand in hand, they walked to the surrey.

Back at the farm, the first thing Alyssa did was to change into her own clothes. Pulling her t-shirt over her head, she was certain she heard a moan from George and Martha's bedroom. Her skin seemed to shrink. Something must be terribly wrong.

She put Martha's dress on a hanger and set her shoes neatly by the wall. Running down the steep stairs in her bare feet she found Deborah, who was on the porch trimming a protesting Frances's hair. "Hold still!" Deborah snapped. "If thee doesn't, I might snip thy ear."

"My hair is good!" Frances wiggled out of Deborah's grasp.

Deborah sighed. "Thee needs a good long nap," she shouted, and ran after her.

Herbert clomped up the wooden porch steps. "When are we eating?" he asked.

"I don't know." Deborah had caught up to Frances and was carrying her back; her face was flushed and her hair was messy.

"When are we eating?" Herbert asked again.

Deborah actually scowled. "Later," she said. "This little miss needs to learn to sit still. I thought to trim her hair before lunch, and now that I've started, I plan to finish."

· This hardly seemed the time to tell Deborah about the scary sound coming from her parents' bedroom. "I'll make sandwiches," Alyssa offered. "Herbert, thee can help me."

"I can help thee?" Herbert was dumbfounded. "Cooking is girls' work!"

"Not at my house. My dad fixes supper all the time."

Suddenly Alyssa had an attentive audience. Frances, amazingly, was holding still. "Daddies don't cook," she said. Deborah, alert to the opportunity, resumed her snipping.

Alyssa repressed a smile. "Mine does," she said. "What's so special about that?"

"Thee comes from such a different time," Deborah said. "For all we know, thee's been on the moon."

Herbert picked up a ladybug that was crawling on his arm. "That's not possible. How could she get away from Earth?"

Was it wrong to tell them about the future? "People — scientists — went to the moon a long time ago, before I was born. They've sent a landing craft, with no people on it, to Mars. And there've been space probes, to take close-up pictures of places like Jupiter and Saturn. And —" In her excitement, Alyssa stumbled over words. "Now they've decided Pluto isn't a planet after all! So there's only eight planets, not nine."

The Clayton children stared at her. "This is more than I can even imagine!" Deborah said. Frances made a dash for the rope swing that hung from one of the trees; Deborah chased after her.

"I'm hungry," Herbert said mournfully.

"Help me fix lunch," Alyssa insisted. "Do you ever have picnics?"

Herbert reluctantly followed her inside, but perked up at the prospect of slicing the bread. Alyssa had trouble finding familiar foods, and then realized the Claytons might not have things like mayonnaise. She kept talking so she wouldn't have to hear noises from upstairs. The woman who'd come before meeting obviously was still here; every now and then her voice came through the ceiling. When there was a burst of laughter, Alyssa relaxed. Maybe the woman had just come to visit. Martha must get bored, in bed all the time.

Looking through cupboards, Alyssa found butter and jam. With no fridge, where would the milk and cheese be? Herbert solved that problem by opening a trap door in the floor and bringing them from a place he called the cool room.

"Where's Eva?" Deborah asked, once everyone had gathered around a blanket spread out near the garden.

Frances's lower lip shot out. "The sandwiches look queer." They *did* look strange and heavy, with their thick, crookedly-cut slices.

"Thee'll eat one just the same." George wrapped a sandwich in a cloth napkin. "Edith Smith likely wants some lunch." He walked back to the house.

Deborah stood up too. "I'll look for Eva," she said. "Frances, thy job is to keep the flies off our picnic. Herbert, thee can pick some new lettuce for us." She ran across the grass almost as if she wanted to escape. Wilfred followed her toward the house.

"I'll look, too," Alyssa said, and headed for the barn. The heavy wooden door creaked as she pulled it open. The feel of dust and straw beneath her bare feet made her think of her shoes, still in the girls' bedroom. It took a few minutes for her eyes to adjust to the dim light. A familiar *meow* came from someplace over her head. "Marigold!" she cried.

Marigold sat on a wooden beam bordering the loft. He meowed again with a lonely sound, and paced his way along, tail twitching behind him.

"Come here, Marigold," she called.

A sniffling sound came from the loft.

"Eva?" When there was no answer, Alyssa started up the ladder. Halfway up, she saw Susannah on a pile of hay. Remembering the talk about Herbert's teasing, she knew what had happened. Rescuing the doll, she went to find Eva.

Eva's face was wet with tears and her shoulders shook uncontrollably.

"Eva, what's wrong?" Alyssa set the doll in her lap, then tentatively put an arm around the girl.

"Mama's terribly sick," Eva choked. "I'm not to go inside. Edith Smith told me so."

So she hadn't imagined the moan. Then why had the women laughed while she and Herbert were making sandwiches? Unless … was Martha Clayton having the baby? Did the others know? What did families do when babies were born at home? They wouldn't just make everybody wait outside, would they?

"Maybe thy mom's having the baby," Alyssa said.

Eva's tense shoulders relaxed. "Oh, thee must be right."

The hay rustled and Marigold stepped into Alyssa's lap. Clutching her cat, she buried her face in his dusty fur. A rumbling purr vibrated along his ribs. Marigold would probably have to stay here. This might be the last time she'd ever hold him.

A small hand reached to stroke Marigold's head. "I like thy puss," Eva said. "He's not half-wild like the other cats."

Alyssa swallowed hard. "Will thee take care of him for me?"

A startled smile flashed across Eva's face. "Yes!"

"The others are looking for you," Alyssa said. "We're having a picnic. Try not to worry about thy mom. I'm sure Edith Smith is taking good care of her."

"Aunt Agnes and Uncle Arthur have invited us to visit this afternoon, before the Fourth of July picnic," George said as lunch finished. "Aunt Tacy is coming to be with Mama for a while."

There was an excited shout from Herbert. Alyssa looked at Deborah; the other girl's mouth was set in a worried line. Alyssa glanced at her jeans and t-shirt, which were smudged with dust. Were they too messy for visiting?

There wasn't time to think about it. After clearing up, Deborah rinsed the dishes in a bucket by the pump and took them inside. Alyssa folded the blanket. Wilfred and Flossie brought the horses from the pasture, and Herbert helped his older brother hitch up the wagon. Alyssa climbed into the big, boxy vehicle. She noticed that Frances was clutching Susannah. Deborah lifted Charles, and then held Eva's hand as they settled.

The horses seemed eager to go. This time they went the opposite direction. It was a bouncy ride, jostling over ruts. Dust washed up around them and didn't go away. Did Iowa still look like this in her time? For an instant an American Painted Lady butterfly alit on the rim of the wagon near Alyssa's arm. A thrill raced through her. The last time she'd seen one was in class, when they raised butterflies from a science project kit.

When they arrived at another farm, two dogs raced to meet them, followed by children of various ages. Alyssa felt comfortably ignored amidst the excited greetings. Some of the girl cousins were wearing jeans — they were old-fashioned and baggy, but definitely jeans.

With so many children milling around, Alyssa couldn't keep track of names. The boys soon vanished, except for Charles. Eva seemed content to keep an eye on him as she and Frances, along with two cousins, sat down to play in a "house" in a treed area. There were several "rooms" with walls defined by borders of piled-up pine needles. "Time to go to bed now," Eva told her little brother. Alyssa watched as Charles cooperatively headed for an old back seat from a car. "No!" a cousin cried. "Charles, thee mustn't go through the wall! The door is here!"

"Let's go to the brook," Deborah said to her cousins Winifred and Reva.

Alyssa cautiously followed them into a hilly pasture, ducking through a barbed wire fence. Barefooted, they walked across the grass. While it looked easy, Alyssa envied them their toughened feet; little prickly things kept sticking to the soles of her feet. Just in time she avoided a thistle that had fallen sideways. At the top of the first hill, one of the cousins lay down on the grass and rolled. Deborah laughed and did the same. Alyssa was left standing there while the others shrieked and laughed, picking themselves up at the bottom. "Alyssa!" Deborah called. "Thee should try it!"

Now the slope looked steeper — and what if there were cow pies? Then she thought of Brooklynne, with her straight, shiny hair, her silver braces, and her perfect shirts. Brooklynne would say "*Ewwww!*" and say mean things about the girls who'd gone down. Rachel would say, "Why not?" and roll. Alyssa lay down. Pushing off, she felt her body gather momentum until she was spinning sideways over grass and wildflowers. At the bottom she lay there, dizzy, watching the sky swirl above her, and breathed in the sweet smells of clover and other flowers. Then she climbed back up the hill to do it again.

The house was no longer in sight; it was just grassy hills with occasional trees and the mooing of cows beneath an expansive sky. Deborah noticed. "Is the bull in this pasture?" she asked warily.

Cousin Reva shook her head. "Daddy put him in the north pasture."

Relieved, Alyssa looked at the cows from their safe distance. For some reason most of them were facing the same direction.

They went over another hill and down again, and then they were approaching a small stream. Deborah ran ahead and sat on a flat rock. Alyssa held back a moment, just looking at Deborah Clayton, her Great-Grandmother Newlin as a girl, with the breeze ruffling the brown hair around her face. She sat quietly, leaning back on her hands, and seemed happy.

The stream — or brook, as Deborah called it — was a mesmerizing place. Alyssa watched minnows flitting beneath the surface. Lying back in the sunny grass, she watched redwing blackbirds flying overhead, listening to their distinctive calls. A wonderfully lazy feeling crept through her.

When the other girls woke her up, it was time for the Fourth of July picnic. But ... it *couldn't* be July fourth! No bands were playing, no fireworks were being shot off, and there weren't even any flags in sight.

Other families had arrived. Blankets were spread on the grass. After a silent grace, everyone shared in a potluck feast of cold fried chicken, salads, sandwiches, and pies. Children ran around; adults ate and visited and, as the sky darkened and the fireflies came out, the men built a bonfire. Someone broke branches off a mulberry tree for a marshmallow roast. Alyssa held her stick over the coals and then licked her fingers after eating the sweet, slightly-blackened treat.

People began singing. Again the songs were familiar, ones Grandma Hadley had sung a long time ago. In the midst of it, Alyssa thought about Martha Clayton having the baby. *Please, God*, she thought as hard as she could, over and over. *Let everything be all right!*

Someone asked Deborah to sing her new song. Alyssa sat there, her skin shivering at the familiar tune and words. Afterwards, there was a moment of silence ... broken by Frances's shriek: "Where's Susannah?"

Not again! Alyssa sighed and got up to help Deborah search. A telltale cloth form dangled upside-down from the mulberry tree. "I see her!" Alyssa called to Deborah. She pulled herself into the tree and crawled out on a strong branch. The orange firelight flickered in the leaves. Wood smoke drifted over her with a change in

the wind. Holding herself steady on the creaking branch,
Alyssa crept out further and grasped the doll.

Suddenly dizzy, she braced herself.

Alyssa fell.

Chapter Eighteen

How could she have been so clumsy? The people below her might get hurt!

The dizziness intensified. Alyssa blinked, but saw only blackness. She thumped down hard.

"Alyssa!"

At the startled exclamation, everything came into focus. The bonfire, the mulberry tree, everyone at the Fourth of July picnic — all of it was gone. Except ...

Beside her on the rug in the baby's room, a face with twinkly black button eyes and a cute little hand-sewn nose and mouth smiled at her. "Oh, no!" she moaned.

"Alyssa, what's wrong?" Mom leaned forward, still holding the picture. "What happened to your hair?"

Clutching Susannah's soft form, Alyssa sat up. Brown yarn braids draped across her arm.

"Where were you this time?" Ethan demanded, before she had a chance to answer Mom. He tossed the magnifying glass from one hand to the other. "You smell like you've been in a forest fire."

Alyssa stood up. "Oh — the bonfire. We were having the Fourth of July picnic ..."

"What?" Ethan looked confused. "It's May, not July."

"It's summer there. We went to meeting in the surrey." She reached for the magnifying glass. "Can I have that? I have to take Susannah back right now." Otherwise, Frances would really throw a fit.

"*Susannah?*" Mom's face went white. She reached for the doll; her hands were cold, and trembled. Mom sagged into the rocking chair, stroking Susannah's hair and tracing the features of her cloth face. Alyssa noticed a smudge of ash on Susannah's arm, and a sticky spot on her skirt, probably from a burnt marshmallow. Tears rolled down Mom's cheeks.

"Mom?" Alyssa gasped.

"I used to play with this doll," her mother whispered.

"Too weird!" Ethan said.

"I used to play with her." Mom's voice was stronger. "By the time I had her, she wasn't in such good shape."

"I have to take her back," Alyssa said reluctantly. "Otherwise Frances will *really* scream." She and George had both agreed it would be best if she didn't go back — but now if she didn't, even for a few minutes, Susannah would truly be lost, and then Mom couldn't possibly be given the doll in the past, when she was a girl.

The photograph of the Claytons was in the box with the baby clothes. Mom must've put it there. When Alyssa picked it up, her heart hammered. The picture seemed cloudy, somehow, the familiar faces less distinct. She glanced at Mom, who was rocking the doll, holding it against her shoulder as if it were a real baby. She turned to Ethan. "Eeth, you've got to help! Otherwise everything'll be messed up."

Ethan grimaced. "What do you want me to do? You missed a whole day of school, you know. Last night Zach wanted to go to a movie — but no, I had to stay here and cover for you. Then Mom found out, so I had to try and explain. Don't you know it's five in the morning?"

Alyssa gasped. "So where's Dad?"

Ethan shrugged. "Asleep, I guess. He had a bunch of meetings yesterday, and didn't get home until really late. I think maybe Mom didn't tell him."

For an instant Alyssa didn't know what to say. Time was running out. She took a deep breath and explained what she wanted Ethan to do.

She ran to her bedroom and grabbed the plastic bag with the thrift store dress for Deborah. In her wastebasket, she rummaged through the discarded clothes and took out the best ones. How much time had passed in Iowa? How were Martha and the baby doing? Then something else crossed her mind. She removed the photo of herself with Marigold from its place at the corner of the mirror. On the back, she wrote:

For Deborah Clayton,
Love from thy great-granddaughter
Alyssa Dixon. July 4, 1931, taken in the
fall of 2006.

As she looked at the print one last time, the other Alyssa smiled at her. So did Marigold. She slipped the photo into her jeans pocket and carried everything to Charlotte's room. Ethan stood impatiently by the crib. Mom, in the rocking chair with Susannah, seemed oblivious.

Alyssa put the dress and her old clothes in her backpack, then frantically scooped as many of Charlotte's baby things as she could into the box. She felt a stab of guilt, looking at the jumble, but there wasn't time to fold.

"Mom," she said softly. "We have to go." She slipped one arm through the strap of her backpack and squeezed into the rocking chair beside Mom, holding the box in her lap. Nodding to Ethan, she tucked her free arm through the crook of her mother's elbow.

Ethan's jaw dropped. "Lyssa! What…?"

"Please?" she said. She reached for the photograph of the Claytons.

Her brother's hand shook as he held the magnifying glass. It was hard to focus on Deborah's face; even worse, it was beginning to look more like just an old picture. "Deborah!" she pleaded.

In the picture, Deborah's eyes seemed to meet hers. Breathing fast, Alyssa thought the words of the song as strongly as she could: *If thee feels sad and all alone …*

A prickly tingling wrapped itself around her. There was a shriek. The rocking chair tipped.

The grass was wet with dew. The summer sky arched high with a celebration of sunrise colours. A rooster

178

crowed. The windmill was creaking and grinding in a slow rotation. Not too far away, cows mooed.

"Oh my God ... *oh my God!*" Mom's hysterical voice cut through the peaceful dawn.

Somewhere, Flossie started barking.

Alyssa sat up and grabbed her mother's arm. "Mom. Shhh! Everything's going to be okay. Calm down. *Please!*"

There was another whimper, but then Mom's jaw tightened. She brushed her stringy hair back from her face.

Alyssa checked for the things she'd intended to bring. Susannah lay on the grass, her braids scattered at a rakish angle. The backpack was still looped over her arm. The box of Charlotte's baby clothes was on its side and some of the tiny sleepers had fallen out. Alyssa pulled the photo out of her jeans pocket. Without looking at it, she tucked it inside the thrift store bag.

They were near the vegetable garden. Judging from the sky, it must be milking time. Would Wilfred and Herbert be out with the cows? Would George come walking by?

Alyssa looked longingly at the house. In the yard, blankets were spread on the grass.... But she shouldn't interfere in the past anymore. Besides, there might not be much time before Ethan picked up the picture.

Mom drew in a sharp breath. "I remember this place!" she whispered. "When I was a really little girl we visited Great-Grandpa and Grandma Clayton!" More tears streamed down her cheeks, but Mom's mouth was smiling. As Alyssa watched, her mother looked around in wonderment.

"Lyssa," Mom said. "Can we walk around, just a little bit?"

Alyssa bit her lip. "I need to get the stuff to the house." Working quickly, she crammed the spilled baby clothes into the box. She emptied her backpack, setting the thrift store bag and the clothes on top of the baby things. Where should she put Susannah?

Hesitating, Alyssa looked around. The garden seemed to beckon. Alyssa set the doll at the base of a healthy bean plant. Susannah's black button eyes seemed to twinkle as she sat there propped up by the green foliage.

Alyssa scooped up the box. With her free hand, she grasped her mother's hand tightly and didn't let go.

Chapter Nineteen

Lying in bed, Alyssa thought about everything that had happened. Although her alarm clock said it was 11:30, she didn't have to worry about school. Mom had phoned to say she and Ethan wouldn't be in class.

She turned over, longing for Marigold's company. Ever since he was a kitten, he'd been a warm, cuddly presence in bed with her. Her throat ached, but she held herself under control — there'd already been more than enough crying, and she was definitely too big to blubber. Eva had promised to take care of Marigold.

By now the Claytons would've found the clothes. She'd left them sitting on the front porch. Someone would've picked up Susannah. Did Deborah have the picture of her? *I'm ever so glad to have a picture of thee!* Alyssa smiled, imagining her voice. What about Martha and the baby?

The real surprise was the change in Mom. Alyssa thought about how she'd looked, rocking Susannah in the chair, and then how her face shone during the short time they'd been at the Claytons' farm. It had been only a few minutes; after depositing the box, they'd walked past the barn. Flossie bounded over. And in the midst of a wet-nosed, tail-wagging greeting, the familiar tingling dizziness swooped them home.

The words of Deborah's song circled in her head. In an uncanny way, the song seemed to tell the story of everything that had been happening. Alyssa hummed and thought about the lines "Find courage in the light within." Had she felt the Inner Light? She wasn't sure, but she'd have to have plenty of courage soon — the next time she saw Brooklynne. Especially now that her only shoes were the pink ones. And when she did her report.

Let thy life shine ... that part of the song made sense; it meant doing her best, and trying to see the good in things. It meant, like George Clayton had said, having faith, and trying to keep love in your heart. It meant act-ing responsibly.

How could she act responsibly about Brooklynne?

No answers came.

With a burst of energy, Alyssa stripped the dirty sheets off her bed and pushed them down the laundry chute. She studied herself in the bathroom mirror. The new short style looked like it belonged in another country. It hadn't mattered at the time, but now ... If kids at school already thought she was a little weird, this would confirm it. She grimaced at her reflection, which grimaced back.

Alyssa tousled her hair. Still it fell into the rather boxy shape. She sighed and reached in the medicine cabinet for the scissors, then snipped cautiously at the sides. There was no noticeable change. She clipped more ruthlessly, and kept going. Now the two sides weren't even. She stepped back for another despairing look. It wasn't as terrible as Frances's haircut, but ... She dropped the scissors in the sink and brushed all the loose hair into the wastebasket.

After a shower she felt clean, but now her hair dribbled in little wet curls. She wound a towel around her head. "Mom?"

"I'm out here." Her mother's voice came from the dining room.

Alyssa found her sitting at the table. Mom had showered too, and she was actually wearing her own clothes for a change. Coloured photos and old black-and-white ones were spread out in front of her.

A shy look crossed Mom's face. "Lyssa," she said, "did I imagine something totally strange this morning?"

Alyssa shook her head. "No." How could they start talking about it? Mom had only seen a little bit of the farm, not the people. She pulled out the chair at Ethan's place and sat down. "Who are you looking at?"

"Family." Mom sighed. "I've let all of you down, *terribly*, these past several months."

Alyssa didn't know what to say, so she rummaged through the pictures. There was one of herself when she was a baby. In another photo, Grandpa and Grandma Hadley were with her and Ethan. It was one of the times they'd all gone camping together, in northern Michigan.

The silence changed; Mom was pulling away, back into the hurt shell. Alyssa took a deep breath. "I think I understand," she said. "It was so sad ..."

183

"That doesn't make it all right." There was a clicking sound as Mom's hand tapped the table top. She was wearing her wedding ring again! The ceiling light glinted off the gold band.

Alyssa began singing Deborah's song; it seemed the right thing to do. In a moment Mom was trying to sing too, but her voice choked. Alyssa stood up and put her arm around Mom's shoulder. Mom clasped her hand.

"I didn't know you knew that song," Mom said faintly, afterwards.

Alyssa swallowed. "I learned it from Deb — from Great-Grandmother Newlin. She made it up, when she was my age." It didn't seem important to talk about the *Stardancer* song. Mom probably didn't even know she'd gone to the movie.

"Did we really…?"

"That's where I was, those other times." Alyssa's heart beat faster. At last, she could talk about it! "You used to play with Susannah?" she asked.

Mom smiled; it was a secret, remembering smile. "Your Grandma Hadley gave her to me. She was old and floppy — and she didn't have braids. Her hair was jaggedy, as if a child had cut it."

Frances! Alyssa started to laugh. "Frances must've done that," she said.

"Great-Aunt Frances? Did you see her?"

Alyssa told Mom about screechy Frances, and how, with Herbert's help, Susannah kept getting lost. Then something occurred to her. "Do you still have Susannah?" she asked. "Can I see her?"

Mom looked away. "No," she said. "I don't have Susannah anymore." There was something she wasn't saying.

The silence stretched out. Alyssa picked up a picture of Mom and Dad when they were just married. "How come?"

"Well, she was old and raggedy." Mom sounded so embarrassed that Alyssa didn't look at her. "Her hair looked really ugly. She had holes in her arms and legs, and the rag stuffing kept coming out. My mother tried fixing her but it didn't look good."

"So what happened?"

"I was fourteen." Mom's voice grew stronger. "My parents wouldn't let me see a movie because they said it was too violent. I was sure everybody else at school had already gone. I had a tantrum, I guess. I grabbed that old doll by the arm and whacked her against the door frame. Eventually she went flying, and all I had left in my hand was her arm."

"You *wrecked* her?"

Mom gave a rueful smile. "I've felt terrible about it ever since. Susannah is buried in the backyard in Indiana, where we used to live."

"Oh." Alyssa slumped in her chair. The towel slid off her head.

"Lyssa —?" Mom's mouth twitched. "What happened?"

Alyssa ran her hands through her wet hair. "It looked too ugly."

"Oh boy …" And Mom actually had the nerve to laugh! After a startled instant, Alyssa helplessly joined in.

"Let's get our hair cut," Mom said. "I've got the exact opposite problem."

"I could cut yours. It'd be cheaper." Alyssa sputtered with laughter.

Mom stood up. "No thanks." As she swished Alyssa's wet hair, she smelled wonderfully clean.

"Have you seen Marigold?" Mom asked. She stood at the kitchen counter tearing up lettuce for the salad. She looked younger with her nice haircut. "Somebody fed him — Ethan, probably — but he hasn't touched his food."

A painful lump blocked Alyssa's throat. She'd already seen the cat bowl, filled with yellowish pellets. "He's in Iowa," she said, dropping the carrot she'd been peeling. "He was in my lap."

Mom's arms came around her, pulling her close. "It'll certainly be a change for him," she said after a while.

"But that was 1931. He's dead now!"

"I guess so." Mom sounded sad; her hand kept stroking Alyssa's short hair. "Come to think of it, there's something I think you'd like to see."

Listlessly, Alyssa followed her back to the dining-room table. The pictures were still spread out. Mom rummaged through them. "I don't remember seeing this one before. It's a little unusual."

The picture in Mom's hand had a cat-claw hole in the upper corner. Alyssa leaned forward to look.

The Claytons were posed in front of their house. Martha was holding a baby! Alyssa sagged with relief. A black-and-white Deborah smiled at her. She was wearing the dress from the thrift shop. "Deborah's wearing the dress I bought! Is that what's unusual?"

"No." Mom turned the picture over to read the names on the back. "Look at Great-Aunt Eva."

Alyssa took the photo from Mom. Like before, Eva was sitting on the bench, next to a grumpy-looking Frances. In Eva's lap was Marigold!

Hungrily, Alyssa looked at the picture: at Marigold, at a smiling Eva, at a mischievous Herbert. At little Charles, at Wilfred, at George and Martha. The baby's face was scrunched, as if she were about to fuss. Always, her eyes returned to Deborah. "I'm so glad to have this picture of thee," she whispered.

"Are you trying to wear that thing out?"

Alyssa jumped at Ethan's voice. "Look!" she said. "There's Marigold!"

Ethan leaned closer. "Nah, it's just a cat."

Alyssa indicated the full cat dish. "You've been feeding him, right? Did you let him outside?"

When Ethan vehemently denied it, Alyssa lifted the bottom of the new shirt Mom had bought her. "See the scratches? Marigold did that. In Iowa."

Ethan turned away. "I'm going to miss that guy," he said. His voice sounded huskier than usual. "In case you're interested, there's a whole bunch of text messages from Rachel."

Chapter Twenty

Nothing seemed quite real as Alyssa walked to school the next morning. Rachel was talking to her again! First her friend had been sick. Then she'd been busy with the music festival, and she'd had some hard performances. When Rachel found the website, she hadn't known what to say. Then her mom pulled her out of school for a few days and started talking about transferring her to Custer Heights Middle School because she didn't want Rachel to be around Brooklynne anymore. Lori didn't think much of Mrs. Fraser either, but Rachel wasn't supposed to talk about that.

Alyssa yawned. She'd been up late working on her genealogy project; finally she'd had an exciting idea. With one more day to go, everything should be ready. If Mrs. Fraser wasn't happy, there wasn't much she could do.

The pink shoes seemed to float over the sidewalk. She studied them critically as one foot, then the other, stepped forward. The new purple laces bounced. A bright blue peace symbol flashed on each foot. When Mom offered to buy her another pair, a strange feeling had welled up inside. Ethan had bought her these shoes. It seemed important that she wear them.

Lawns were green everywhere she looked, and the sun was warm on her bare arms. Trees were leafing out. Tulips and other bright flowers bloomed around people's houses. Birdsong and traffic sounds drifted through the spring air. Her very ordinary neighbourhood seemed ... strange. Somehow she kept expecting to see cornfields, and wildflowers along the roadside.

Regret tugged at her. She'd never be able to go back to Deborah's time. At least, it wouldn't be right to try. The baby, Alice Emma, was safely born. Deborah — Great-Grandmother Newlin — was very old now, but she was still alive. So were Herbert, Frances, Charles, and Alice.

Alyssa dug in her backpack for the letter. When it appeared in the mailbox yesterday, addressed to her in Great-Grandmother Newlin's spidery handwriting, she'd needed to sit down to open it. Inside, there'd been a letter to Mom, and another sealed envelope. The envelope read:

To my dearest Alyssa,

You may think this an unusual request, but I would ask that you keep this envelope sealed until a time when your hair is short, and you have had a most remarkable experience. That time must be quite near, so if you don't understand just now, I hope you can be patient.

189

When Alyssa opened the envelope, she found another letter — and the picture of herself holding Marigold! It looked old now, with the edges battered and worn. There was a sticky note on the back, with the same elderly script: "Thee will likely enjoy having this back. It has been a treasure during these many years."

The second letter, in rounded, girlish handwriting, was dated July 10, 1931. Walking to school, Alyssa read it again:

Dear Alyssa,

I feel very strange, writing thee a letter I cannot send, yet I feel that I must. Thee cannot begin to imagine how wonderful it was to have thee here! Imagine — meeting my own great-granddaughter, and here I am, not quite twelve years old! I thank thee for the pretty dress! (The bag is made of the oddest material.)

Though I tried hard not to show it, when Mama was sick I felt overwhelmed by so much work. There were many times when I simply wished to curl up and sleep, or to shout at everyone, or perhaps even run away! Thy being here gave me something more to think about, and someone to talk to. It helped me be more patient and, I hope, more loving. I feel dreadful, having held such thoughts in my heart!

Baby Alice is with us now, and she is a strong little girl. Mama was overwhelmed by thy gift. The clothes would have been for thy dear sister Charlotte, I am thinking. We don't know the names for some of these items, and it is rather queer when we try to explain about them! Thy family will be glad to know that they are of great help.

Mama was so sick. We feared that she might grow worse, and that perhaps both Mama and the baby might be lost. Before thee came, Frances had a habit of running upstairs at every opportunity. Mama's condition involved terrible headaches. Though Mama would never admit it, I know our noisy Frances sometimes puts her at her wits' end. Thank thee for helping keep Frances busy. And poor, dear Susannah! Now Frances has cut her braids off! She looks horridly wild and uncared for. Mama put such loving work into our doll, and I haven't the heart to bring Susannah to her.

Thee will be glad to know that Eva loves thy Marigold dearly. Since thee was here, she smiles more often.

Sometimes we hear her laugh and sing. I can tell thee this next thing because thee certainly cannot tell Mama. Sometimes Eva dresses her new puss in clothes for the baby! He squirms and protests, but seems to understand that my sister is a loving soul who needs special care.

I have written down the words for our song so that we will always have them.

Herbert thanks thee for the shirts. He cannot understand, though, why a boy would wear a pink shirt, and others with flowers?

I hear baby Alice squalling. Mama still needs her rest, so I must stop for now.

I can hardly wait for the time when I will see thee again! Thee never did tell me whom I will marry! I suppose I shall have to find that out for myself.

Hoping that thee may always walk in the Light, and with love,

Thy Deborah

Alyssa nearly tripped on a crack in the sidewalk as she reread Deborah's words. Really, it was a miracle!

Mocking laughter came from across the street. "Look at the geek — studying on the way to school."

Brooklynne! Mackenzie was there too. Alyssa's insides froze. Whatever happened, she couldn't let them see the letter. She folded it quickly and zipped it in her backpack. Because she knew she must, she walked across the street and faced the other girls.

Brooklynne's hazel eyes looked at her with derision. Her upper lip curled into a sneer. "What do you want, loser?"

Words wouldn't come, but Alyssa knew she couldn't back down. Trembling, she stared straight at Brooklynne's hard eyes.

"Well, say something. We're not going to be late because of a dumb loser." Brooklynne made as if to brush past, but slammed hard against her at the last minute.

Alyssa gasped at the impact. With it, words came. "So now you're getting physical," she said, catching up to stand directly in Brooklynne's way. "What have you got against me? It's not like I do anything to you."

Brooklynne's gaze fell on the pink shoes. "Hey, cool shoes." Her voice was ripe with sarcasm. "Where'd you get them?"

Alyssa drew in a deep breath. "In a store." Her fists clenched at her sides. In the distance, the warning bell sounded at school.

The other girls didn't seem to notice. "Look at her new hairstyle," Mackenzie said.

"Who cut it?" Brooklynne jeered. "Your grandma?"

"Actually, it was my great-grandmother." Alyssa sucked in another breath. Unless she did something, they'd keep right on sniping at her. There was only one

193

way she could think of to take control. "You know, that website was really evil. My brother wanted to tell the newspaper. *And* the TV station. I don't think the mayor would be quite as popular if everybody knew what his kid does." The shaking was deep inside now and wouldn't quit.

Brooklynne's face reddened. "So why didn't you tell, huh?"

"There are better ways." What ways, she had no idea, but Brooklynne couldn't read her mind.

Brooklynne shrieked with laughter. Sunlight glinted off her braces. "Like what? Praying?" In a blinding instant, something stomped hard on her foot. Fingernails clawed her cheek.

"*Brooklynne!*" Mackenzie yelped.

"I feel sorry for you," Alyssa forced herself to say through the pain. There was a stunned silence, then the sound of running footsteps.

Alyssa took her time going the rest of the way to school. For a while she could feel blood trickling down her cheek.

In the office, as she waited for Mr. Bergman to finish talking to a parent, she flipped through the phone book. With shaking hands, she dialed the mayor's office at City Hall. "Wes Bayne," said a strong, confident voice at last. "How can I help you?"

"This is Alyssa Dixon." She felt freezing cold. "Your daughter Brooklynne assaulted me on the way to school today. She also put up a hate website about me a couple of weeks ago. We have copies of everything."

There was a blank silence at the other end of the line. Alyssa realized that the school office was silent too.

"Excuse me," Mr. Bergman said to somebody else. "We've got an emergency here. I'll phone you later, Mrs. Nordstrom."

"Are you at school now?" said the voice in the receiver. "I'll be there right away."

Alyssa leaned heavily against the counter. "Could you call my mom?" she asked, and burst into tears.

At morning recess the next day, Alyssa stood in front of the mirror in the girls' bathroom. "I look ugly." The scratches on her cheek were still painful, and the one closest to her eye was puffy. She tugged at the waist of Deborah's dress. The floor tiles were cool beneath her bare feet. "Rache, what if Mrs. Fraser doesn't like my presentation?"

"She will," Rachel said. "You're wearing authentic clothes. You're doing so much — Mrs. Fraser can't possibly give you a bad grade. My report was so boring she looked like she was falling asleep."

Apprehension knotted Alyssa's middle. It wasn't just Mrs. Fraser. For some reason Mr. Bergman had decided to listen to the presentations too. "Mrs. Fraser didn't look sleepy," she said. "She was just listening." Her voice echoed off the green-and-grey walls.

A younger girl came into the restroom and gave Alyssa a curious look.

Alyssa turned away. She held a cold wet paper towel

195

against her smarting cheek, then put her school clothes into her backpack. The bell rang.

The classroom was silent when she and Rachel went in. The power point projector was set up. The painting from Alyssa's living room sat in the chalkboard tray beside Rachel's clarinet. Avoiding Mrs. Fraser's eyes, Alyssa walked to the front of the room.

"My name is Deborah Clayton," she said. "I'm Alyssa Dixon's great-grandmother and live on a farm near Chatham, Iowa, in 1931. You might think a bully scratched my face, but we had a vicious rooster. He got the best of me yesterday, so my brothers Wilfred and Herbert butchered him. We ate him for supper."

Cautiously, she made eye contact. Everyone was listening. Brooklynne was conspicuously absent. And, there in the back, were Mom and Dad!

Taking a deep breath, Alyssa continued: "Most people have ordinary lives. But that doesn't mean they're not important." Clicking the remote, she said, "This is my mother, Martha Clayton. She worked hard all her life and raised eight children. One of them died of polio." She told about how George, and then later Wilfred and Charles, farmed the land and donated what little profits they earned to feed hungry families in Appalachia and other places. "One way to help protect freedom is to make sure everybody has enough to eat," Alyssa said. She showed pictures of Herbert as a boy, and later as a man, on crutches with part of one leg missing. "This is my brother Herbert Clayton. In the Second World War he worked for the Quaker ambulance service in France.

He never shot at anybody or hurt anyone, but he got part of his leg blown off. He almost died while helping people."

She went on to talk about Frances, a lively lady who'd helped keep people from taking advantage of those who were mentally ill. She showed a picture of Eva and picked up the painting that had hung in their living room for as long as she could remember. "My sister Eva was very shy," she said. "She loved animals. She was artistic, and painted this picture." Looking down at it, at the animal tracks in the snow — and a cat that looked amazingly like Marigold sitting on top of a fence post — Alyssa pushed back another wave of wonderment. She went on to talk about Alice, and how she'd become a nurse. "I became a teacher," she finally said. "I taught in small country schools and really enjoyed working with the children. I wrote a song, too." She clicked the remote one last time, and the words to Deborah's song came on the screen.

While Rachel played it on her clarinet, Alyssa sang to the class.

Chapter Twenty-One

The phone rang again. Alyssa glared at it. Only a minute ago, Brooklynne had phoned. She'd called Alyssa an extremely rude name and then hung up. Probably now she'd thought of some other awful thing to say. Mackenzie had said that Brooklynne was suspended from school for a week. Couldn't she think of anything better to do?

Mom was vacuuming, so she wouldn't hear the phone. Ethan was playing soccer with Zach and some other boys. Dad was at the college.

The phone kept ringing. Alyssa sighed and picked it up. "Hello?"

"Is that Alyssa?" It was a man's voice.

"Yes," she said cautiously.

"It's Warren Stanley," he continued. "A while ago you asked about going to another peace march. There will be one this Saturday, downtown. Are you still interested?"

"Um, yes." It had been a while since she'd thought about the war.

"Great!" Warren Stanley said. "If anyone in your house needs a ride, just let me know."

After hanging up, Alyssa turned on the news channel. A journalist in the Middle East had been kidnapped. There were shots of helicopters flying over poor villages. Somebody who worked for an oil company insisted the war had nothing to do with America wanting more oil. Alyssa almost walked away, but then a commercial for fertilizer came on. The picture showed wide open fields of green wheat. It didn't look that different from Iowa....

It had been so long since the family had gone out of town. "Mom?" she yelled when the vacuum cleaner stopped. "Can we go to that reunion?"

Mom came out to the living room. Her new hairstyle, with its highlights, made her look perky. "I've been thinking about it," she said. "Dad can't go. He'll be teaching a summer course, and Ethan's already signed up for soccer camp. But you and I could go."

"Yay!" Elated, she ran to give Mom a hug. "Oh, Warren Stanley phoned. There's going to be a peace march on Saturday. Want to go?"

Mom smiled. "Sorry. I have so much catching up to do around this place. When I start teaching again I want everything in good shape. Actually, what I plan to do this Saturday is to clean out —" her voice faltered. "— the spare room. You can go if you'd like. Maybe Rachel and Lori will be interested."

There hadn't been enough time to make another poster. Rachel was carrying their old one. Walking beside her, Alyssa felt so light in her pink shoes that she almost imagined she could fly. She made herself walk steadily, but she really wanted to dance in the buoyant pink shoes.

"How come you're in such a good mood?" Rachel asked.

"Because."

"Because your mom's better? Because of your report? Or is it because Brooklynne got suspended?" Rachel's frizzy hair bounced as she walked. All around them were the sounds of talking, walking feet, and a pair of tapping drumsticks that echoed off the buildings.

Alyssa shrugged. "All of it." Yes, Mom was better. And Mrs. Fraser had given her an A+ for her genealogy project. It might have had something to do with Mr. Bergman listening to the presentations, but one way or the other, now she'd be giving the presentation again — in front of the whole school. Yes, it was nice having Brooklynne gone from class for a while, but the really important thing was that she'd stood up to Brooklynne, and had told Brooklynne's dad and Mr. Bergman. She'd done it herself, instead of depending on Mom or Dad to do it for her.

"What do we want?" yelled the man with the megaphone.

"*PEACE!*" everybody else yelled.

"When do we want it?"

"*NOW!*"

When it was quieter, Rachel persisted, "Because *what?*"

"Because you're still my friend. And because now I feel like I'm in a whole big family," she continued. "Before, it was like just us, and once in a while we'd visit relatives, or they'd come see us. Now I really know where I came from — part of me, anyhow." Probably she should thank Mrs. Fraser too, because without that assignment, she might not have paid as much attention.

Rachel's mom Lori was walking with Warren Stanley, whose white hair waved in the breeze. "Let's walk with them." Alyssa darted ahead and fell in step with Warren. "Thank you for phoning," she said to him.

Warren Stanley smiled.

And then Alyssa noticed the TV camera. A photographer had it aimed right at Warren Stanley, and now at her too. Walking beside the photographer was Brooklynne's mom. Crystal Bayne had the same hard, polished look that Brooklynne had. She didn't seem particularly happy to be talking to people at the march, but she was doing her job anyhow. She asked Warren Stanley some questions. When he talked about the importance of justice and mercy, and truth and peace and true freedom for all people, Alyssa's heart glowed.

"I'm going to be on the news!" Alyssa yelled as soon as she got home. She ran down the hall, stopping in the doorway of the baby's room.

Except it *wasn't* a baby's room anymore. The crib and some of the other furniture were gone; so were the teddy bear mobile and the pictures from the walls. The rocking chair was still there. Alyssa sat in it and looked at the cheerful orange butterflies on the curtains.

Ethan poked his head through the doorway. "You're going to be on the news? Cool!"

"Mostly Warren Stanley," Alyssa said. She held out her feet, with the pink shoes. "These are perfect peace march shoes," she said.

Ethan shrugged and came into the room. "I like my bedroom downstairs way better. I hope they let me keep it."

Alyssa rocked harder; there was a comforting squeak each time the chair went backwards. "Mom's been calling this the 'spare room.' They probably won't make you move."

"So," Ethan said. "What do you think made Mom snap out of it like she did?"

"I dunno." Alyssa had thought about it several times. "Maybe it had something to do with that old doll." Alyssa told her brother how Mom had wrecked Susannah when she was his age. "And just *being* there. Mom remembered that place!"

It had been such a shock for Mom. Maybe she'd finally been ready to move ahead after mourning the loss of Charlotte. Alyssa's throat tightened. *She* probably still had some grieving to do. When Charlotte was born dead it was really sad, but she never thought it would change her life in such a big way. Maybe she'd been terribly wrong. That little kicking person who'd jiggled Mom's pregnant stomach had been her sister.

"Hey." Ethan jostled one of her pink shoes. "Earth to Planet Alyssa. If you're going to be on the news, we should turn on the TV. I want to record it."

"Hello?" Dad came in from teaching his Saturday class. He sounded tired.

Alyssa went to meet him. "How was your class?" she asked.

Dad gave her a rueful smile. "Hey there, gorgeous. Do you really want to know?" He ruffled her hair. It used to bother her when her hair was long, but now it felt like a friendly thing to do.

Alyssa scrutinized her father. He no longer looked tense, the way he had during the past several months. "Yes," she decided. "I want to know."

Dad winked at her. "If my students put in even half as much creativity as you did for your assignment, I'd be happy."

Ethan stuck his head out of the spare room. "Lyssa's going to be on the news — and Warren Stanley too."

Alyssa grimaced. "Brooklynne's mom interviewed Warren Stanley. I bet they'll only show a tiny bit of it— especially since he said really good things."

Dad's arm came around her shoulder. "It doesn't matter. The important thing is that the TV station was actually there to cover the march."

Alyssa heard Mom's footsteps coming up the basement stairs. "What's up?" Mom asked.

Everyone started talking at the same time.

Mom gestured helplessly. "Hold on a minute!" She turned to Alyssa. "What's this about TV?"

When they all sat down together to watch the news, the glowing feeling flooded back into Alyssa's heart. She wasn't sure if it was the Inner Light, but she *was* sure that, somehow, she'd found a way to let her life shine.

$\mathcal{E}$pilogue

Alyssa's ears popped as the plane descended. Rivers glinted in the gently rolling green expanse below them. One in particular looped back and forth in such a winding ribbon that it seemed confused. White stripes across the land must be roads.

Exhilaration soared through Alyssa, making her wish she could push through the window and parachute down. Except then she wouldn't land anywhere near the right place.

Mom patted her knee. "You're excited. I am too, actually."

It had been nice of Dad to suggest that they fly. They'd come a day early so there would be time to explore.

The plane swooped lower yet. Des Moines came into sight.

Alyssa tried to memorize everything as their rental car headed west on the interstate. They would be staying in

Adams because Chatham had no motels, and the Middle Raccoon River Meetinghouse was completely out in the country. Through the window Alyssa saw cornfields and pastures. When they crossed a bridge that said Middle Raccoon River, she drew in an excited breath.

It was too early to go to their motel. Looking through tourism guides they'd picked up at the airport, Alyssa found the turnoff for the covered bridges of Madison County. In the little towns along the way, cheerful hollyhocks bordered many of the buildings. The countryside looked so much like what she'd seen in 1931! Masses of wildflowers bloomed by the roadsides. Some of the fence posts were made from crooked tree trunks. When they found the dark red bridges with interesting names, built in the late 1800s, Alyssa shivered. These bridges were there long before Deborah was born … and before George and Martha were born, too!

Walking around with Mom, taking pictures with the digital camera, Alyssa felt as if she'd come home. With wildflowers everywhere, birds singing, and insects flying over the slow-moving river, these places had the same wondrous feeling as the day when she and Deborah went to the brook with the cousins. That had been seventy-six years ago! It was so hard to believe that Deborah was now an old woman.

They watched a glorious sunset outside their motel in Adams. As the sky darkened and the first stars came out, fireflies darted above the freshly cut grass.

"You're quiet, Lyssa," Mom remarked.

Alyssa drew in a long, satisfied breath. "I'm just so happy!"

In the distance came the sounds of firecrackers. The flag flapped on the flagpole outside the motel. It was the Fourth of July — Great-Aunt Alice's birthday. Tomorrow, at the reunion, she and Deborah would meet again.

A gravel road took them north of the interstate. Looking backwards, Alyssa watched white dust billowing behind their car. The fields were green, and cattle and horses grazed. Tall trees grew around the scattered farmhouses and barns, some of which looked no different from ones she'd seen in 1931. Sometimes old farm equipment sat in fields, or near outbuildings. "I feel like I'm in a time warp!" she said to Mom. "It was almost exactly like this! Except, the cars and trucks and tractors are all new."

A small painted sign in a field, nearly obscured by tall grassy weeds, pointed the direction to the Middle Raccoon River Meetinghouse. Alyssa discovered that she was holding her breath. Some of the same trees were there. Bright orange lilies and hollyhocks still bloomed outside the meetinghouse. The building had been painted recently, and there was a ramp for wheelchairs. A new sign said MIDDLE RACCOON RIVER FRIENDS MEETING.

As soon as Mom stopped the car, Alyssa bailed out. Behind the meetinghouse, the Friends school building was gone. But the same grassy area was there, as well as a swing set, a simple wooden play structure, and a climbing apparatus made of tractor tires. Alyssa ran across the grass and launched herself in a crazy, dizzying arc on one of the swings. She laughed out loud, then dragged her feet to stop.

Mom stood in the middle of the grassy area. The breeze ruffled her hair around her face. "Shall we look inside the meetinghouse?" she suggested.

"Yes." Alyssa raced over to Mom and twirled her around in a breathless hug. Together, they tiptoed into the quiet building.

It was the same. On the women's side, Alyssa sat on the bench where she'd sat with Deborah and Eva that morning. Outside the window, green cornfields spread out to the rolling horizon. Then she got up and went to sit on the men's side where she'd sat with George, and they'd talked. Dust motes glowed in a shaft of sunlight. The new homemade cushions were softer, but almost everything really did seem unchanged.

"You really were here," Mom said softly.

Looking at her mother's face, Alyssa decided that the only word that could describe her expression was "awe."

Clumping footsteps sounded on the porch. Alyssa turned around to see who was coming in.

An old man stood in the doorway, leaning on a cane. One of his legs moved in a way that didn't seem natural. "Hello there," he said. "Did you folks just arrive?"

Alyssa stood up. At the same time, Mom said, "Uncle Herbert?"

Alyssa held back. How could that old man shuffling toward them be Herbert?

"Jennifer," he said. "It's good to see you. Deb said you'd be coming." He turned to Alyssa. "And thee surely is Alyssa. Thee looks no different than thee did when I was eight years old!" His hearty laugh loosened the nervous place in Alyssa's stomach.

She hugged him.

Herbert Clayton's gnarled hand stroked her hair for a moment. Then he stepped back to look at her with alert brown eyes. "As I recall, thee brought me some unusual shirts." His wink made Alyssa smile. "I also recall that Debbie was concerned because thee'd left thy shoes." He regarded the pink shoes with their purple laces, blue peace symbols, and the marker designs that obscured the word she'd written that frustrated day. "And what has thee got now?"

Alyssa laughed self-consciously. "I decorated them," she said. "It's good to see ... *thee*, Uncle Herbert."

"Who's here?" called a woman's strident voice. "Are you folks from Illinois?"

"It's the rental car," Alyssa said. "We're from —" She stared at the brisk old woman with pinkish-orange hair. "Frances?" she whispered.

"Look who we've got here!" Herbert said. But there wasn't time for introductions because eight or nine adults and children followed Great-Aunt Frances in — clearly members of her family — and many of them were talking.

Mom stepped forward, clutching her purse. "Is there anything we can do to help?" she asked.

Great-Uncle Herbert took her arm. "Don't worry, Jenny. The folks here have everything organized. Your mother should be arriving soon. She's bringing Deb and Allie. Why don't you sit out on the porch and wait for them." He turned to Alyssa. "And thee, Alyssa — thee'll want to sit with thy mother."

And so she went outside with Mom. The day was hot, but the shade helped. Flies buzzed around, landing on her sweaty arms. More people arrived; Mom didn't speak, so they must be distant relatives.

And then a familiar blue Honda drove down the dusty driveway.

Alyssa's heart sped up. "Grandma's here!" she said. Without waiting for Mom, she ran down the steps and opened the car door for Grandma Hadley.

"Alyssa!" said Grandma. "You look wonderful!" She stepped out and pulled Alyssa into a tight hug. "You've grown up a lot, my girl," she said. "Your parents have talked so much about you. Your dad says you're the one who brought your mother out of her slump. I can't begin to thank you enough."

"I didn't do anything, much." Even so, she leaned against her grandmother. And then she remembered. "Is…?"

Grandma gave her a squeeze. "There's someone here who can't wait to see you."

Shyly, Alyssa walked around to the other side of the car. In the back seat, an elderly woman was unbuckling herself. But that couldn't be Great-Grandmother Newlin; it must be Great-Aunt Alice. Alyssa gave her a quick smile, and then opened the front passenger door.

Her grand-grandmother had a wrinkled, smiling

face with clear grey eyes behind glasses. Her white hair was brushed back from her forehead and held in place by metal clips. It shone in the sunlight. "Alyssa, dear," the old woman said, and reached to clasp her hand.

"Deb — um, Great-Grandmother Newlin!" Alyssa helped her step out of Grandma's car. She couldn't think what to say. Great-Grandmother Newlin was thin and frail, and leaned on her arm.

The flash of a camera made Alyssa blink. Standing nearby, Great-Uncle Herbert had just taken a picture of them.

"Thank thee so much for thy letter," Alyssa said impulsively. "It's wonderful! And thanks for sending the picture. It came only a couple of days after I gave it to thee."

Deborah Clayton Newlin laughed. "And I got to enjoy it for most of a lifetime," she said. "I thank *thee*, Alyssa, for thinking of me and bringing thy picture and that dress — and, most importantly, thyself." She drew back and gave Alyssa an earnest look. "If thee could spare some time to talk with an old lady while thee's here, I would so love to hear more about thy life."

"Say 'cheese,'" said Mom's voice.

Alyssa put her arm around her great-grandmother's waist and smiled.

"That's perfect!" said Grandma Hadley.

Mom's camera flashed.

More Great Fiction for Young People

Growing Up Ivy
by Peggy Dymond Leavey
978-1554887231
$12.99 £7.99

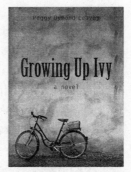

Living in grim Depression-era Toronto with her actress mother, Frannie, Ivy Chalmers has never met her father. In 1931, Frannie sends twelve-year-old Ivy to stay with her paternal grandmother in Larkin, Ontario, while she seeks stardom in New York City. When Ivy's father, Alva, arrives unexpectedly in Larkin, he turns out not to be the Prince Charming she imagined, but an illiterate peddler. Rescuing Ivy from her uncompromising grandmother, Alva takes her with him for the summer, wandering the countryside by horse-drawn caravan, selling shoes.

Back in Larkin at summer's end, Ivy meets teenager Charlie Bayliss, orphaned as an infant and raised by his aunt on a farm outside town. Ivy has a flair for writing and boundless imagination, while Charlie loves baseball and loathes farming. Unknown to both of them, though, is a secret connection they share. When the final pieces of the puzzle of their lives fall into place, nothing will ever be the same.

Kootenay Silver
by Ann Chandler
978-1554887552
$12.99 £7.99

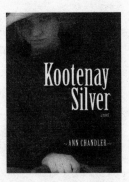

In 1910, while twelve-year-old
Addy McLeod waits in a cabin
in the Kootenay wilderness of
southeastern British Columbia
for her brother, Cask, to send for her, she fends off the
unwanted advances of her alcoholic stepfather. When
tragedy strikes, she is forced to flee and disguise herself as a boy.

Addy's determined search for Cask becomes
a journey of self-discovery as she encounters a tough
trapper woman who cares for her when she's ill, works
in a hotel in the silver town of Kaslo on Kootenay Lake,
and meets her first love, Ian.

But just as Addy's search for Cask is about to
end, the First World War breaks out and her world is
torn apart once again. With great resolve she devotes
herself to joining the war effort on the home front and
eventually learns what forgiveness is all about.

Available at your favourite bookseller.

DUNDURN
www.dundurn.com

What did you think of this book? Visit www.dundurn.com for reviews, videos, updates, and more!